The Under The Stairs

ADAM G NEWTON

This book is a work of fiction. Names, characters, places
and incidents are products of the author's imagination or
are used fictitiously. Any resemblance to actual events
or locales or persons, living or dead, is entirely
coincidental.

First Printing, 2014

ISBN: 150306591X
ISBN-13: 978-1503065918

Cover designed by Adam G Newton.

http://www.adamgnewton.co.uk

"All the world's a stage, and all the men and women merely players: they have their exits and their entrances; and one man in his time plays many parts, his acts being seven ages."

- *William Shakespeare*

All the characters portrayed in this story are fictitious, but like all good stories, they might just be based on real people.

If you think one of them might be based on you, then congratulations. Told you I was going to make you famous.

This is for everyone who still believes.

Act I

ADAM G NEWTON

Chapter 1

It was late on this particular Friday evening, and all the kids had gone home. Bentley Hill Community Hall stood empty save for the single solitary figure of Dave Sweet. *Every week*, Dave thought, *they seem to get later*. Not that Dave minded. There was nothing for him to go home to, other than a worn-out armchair and late night TV, so hanging around until after half past ten to clean up afterwards wasn't a problem.

Dave flipped his brush over, and adjusted the head. For a moment, the casual observer might have been tricked in to thinking there were two copies of Dave, one slightly wider that the other. They say that over time, owners starts to look like their dogs (or vice versa, depending on how you look at it). This held true for Dave too, but he didn't own a dog. He owned a brush.

Tall and thin, with large amounts of brown hair sticking almost straight out, the brush was almost indistinguishable from Dave. The clearest way to tell them apart was that the brush had straight hair, whilst Dave's hair had tight curls.

And possibly more important to whomever may be looking, Dave was dressed in blue overalls, but the brush remained naked.

Dave swept the wooden floor of the hall, first this way, then that. He picked up the empty cans, the empty wrappers, and whatever else was left behind. He took his time, and did his job well. By the time Dave was done in the main room, it was rapidly approaching midnight.

The wind blew outside, and the windows of the hall rattled. Dave began to hurry, as he never liked to be there when the witching hour arrived. He sprinted up the steps on to the stage, glanced around quickly, decided it looked clean, and ran back down the steps. He sped across the hall and out through the doors in to the entrance area. He threw open the storage cupboard door and stashed his brush away amongst all the other cleaning equipment.

BEEP BEEP

Dave's watch told him that he was too late.

A loud creaking came from the main hall,

followed by a tremendous bang. Dave jumped, and ran for the front door. Behind him, he could hear a voice softly speaking. He opened the door, leapt outside, and slammed the door behind him. He fumbled for the keys, and secured all three locks on the outside of the door with shaking hands.

He tried the handle to make sure, and ran as quickly as he could down the front path to the street, taking a left to make his way home. He ran all the way.

And behind him, he could still hear the voice.

"...in the toilet. Look in the toilet. Look in the toilet. Dammit man, look in the toilet!"

ADAM G NEWTON

Chapter 2

Earlier that very same evening, Jim Butler sat in his living room with his wife, Anne. Jim was deeply concerned. During his working life, he'd been good at what he did, but never had to dip too far into the financial side of things. Having worked as a vet for over 40 years, there were many things he *did* have to dip deeply into, but money wasn't one of them.

"We can't go on, Anne. It's finished. There's barely enough money left for painting the sets, let alone anything else!"

Jim's long-suffering wife Anne knew this game. She could agree with Jim, and she could say there was no money. No set would be painted, no clothing purchased, no play. Alternatively, she could state her disagreement. After all, there would be ticket sales, and surely that would cover most of the costs. But in the end, it all depended on how long she wanted Jim to go on for. If she agreed, he would sit and sulk awhile, quietly. She could get on with the dusting or changing the bed sheets or something - *anything* - to get her out of the room. Or she could express hope that the ticket sales would be high, which would result in an hour-long lecture about how the "younger generation" of "iPhone-wizards" would rather spend their time watching "videos on Your Tubes" or "Facing Books" than paying to watch a bunch of fools prance around on stage.

"You know, you're right. There's no money, we won't sell any tickets, there's no point. Now, I need to do the dusting, so you just sit there and think about it, and I'll..."

"Why wouldn't we sell any tickets?"

"What? You know why! The younger wizards of the iPhone generation, or whatever you always say. They don't want to look at your tubes."

"Mmmph."

Jim's grunt was the usual signal for Anne to leave before he said something they might both regret. She got to her feet, and crossed the room to the door, stopping to look back at Jim. He sat brooding in his armchair, with his bald head creased in concentration, ruffling the tufts of almost-white hair that remained just behind his ears. This hair poked out much too far, drawing attention to the fact that the rest of his head was hairless, apart from his eyebrows.

Jim reached for his glasses, which were hung around his neck on a thin piece of string. The string was entirely unnecessary whilst he was sitting down, as the glasses rested comfortably on his ample belly.

"I'm going to look at the numbers again, but this time with less conservative ticket sales. Put the kettle on, love."

Anne turned towards the kitchen and rolled her eyes to the heavens.

"Yes, dear."

***

"Animal magnetism, that's what it is. Girls cannot resist me. Fighting 'em off with a stick, me."

Christopher Crumple sat in the window of the small pizza restaurant opposite his best friend, Harry. Harry was puzzled.

"If you're fighting them off with a stick, why are you sitting here on a Friday night with me?"

"Loyalty, I suppose. Plus, it was your turn to buy."

"So your heart can be won for the price of a pizza?"

"You're putting words in my mouth now..."

"I don't think there's room with the amount of pizza in there. How about you finish chewing before you say anything else, eh?"

Harry was a good few years older than Christopher, but shared the same enthusiastic, boyish outlook on life. But when Christopher's twenty years of life-experience failed, Harry was happy to pull rank and offer his own advice. Especially if the advice required was about women, motorbike maintenance, or chewing with your mouth closed.

"Well, to be honest Harry, *your food* is putting me off *my* food."

"Och, what's wrang wi' ma food?" said Harry, slipping into an exaggerated Scottish accent.

"You know how I feel about tuna on pizza. Fish is for eating with chips, not pizza."

"Aye laddy, soon ye'll be seein' ma haggis on a pizza, then ye'll be sorry."

"Don't ever offer to show me your Haggis. That just sounds wrong. Shut your mouth and eat your food."

"Ah!", said Harry, accent-free. "Now you're getting it!"

They sat quietly for awhile, munching.

"You know, I was talking to Jim yesterday," said Harry. "He said the Players are going to do another show, but it might be their last. Are you up for it?"

"You know I am! Who else is going to be in it?"

"Oh right, I see where your priorities lie. Not, *what's it going to be*? Or, *when is the first read-through*? But, *who's in it*? Why, who do you have your eye on now? Do you have a big enough stick to beat them off with?"

"I think you're getting the wrong end of the stick, mate! It's not like that! I'm in it for the drama, the action. But really, who else is in it?"

"Spill it. who?"

"Sophie."

"Sophie? Mmm. I approve. She's perfect for you."

"What's that supposed to mean?"

"Nothing."

"Harry, if you've got something to say, say it."

"Well, it's just that I don't want you to embarrass yourself like last time. I don't think you should have asked that Lucy girl out on a date. Or at least, not in front of everyone. On opening night."

"It's called bravery, pal."

"It's called stupidity, or at least that's how it came across when she said no."

"I know, right? How stupid of *her*!"

"I meant you."

"Oh. Will Lucy be there this time?"

"No. Didn't you hear? Her dad took a job in Manchester. They've moved!"

"What?! She didn't even tell me!"

"Are you surprised?"

"...no."

"Exactly. So far, it's Jim and Anne, you and me, Sophie, Lillian..."

"...she is *so* old..."

"...don't be cheeky. Lillian, Owen,

and...actually, best not mention it."

"What?"

"Nothing."

"Stop saying that! Who is it?"

"Zoe."

"Zoe? Wow. Primary target acquired."

"She is not for you. No touchy, young man."

"That's what she said."

"Yes, she probably did. Leave it. If you upset her, then you upset her dad. We went through this months ago, the first time she was in one of the shows. She, and her father, are a particular apple cart that does not need upsetting."

"Huh? Apple tart?"

"Her dad owns the hall. He could stop us using it, *just like that*. Are you even listening to me?"

"Not really, sorry. Just thinking about Zoe."

"Well, stop it! What about Sophie?"

"Who?"

ADAM G NEWTON

Chapter 3

Sophie Patterson looked in the mirror, critically studying her own reflection. She looked at her fashionable flat shoes, her tight fitting denim jeans, her plain white short-sleeved crop top that exposed her belly button, her cascading wavy brown hair, her elegant chin, and her pretty smile, Her attention finally settled on the pair of thick glasses resting on her nose.

Sophie was generally happy with her appearance, but decided that her glasses were not adding to the effect, so she removed them.

Sophie Patterson looked in the mirror, trying desperately to see her own reflection. She looked at the dark blur of her shoes, the blue blur above them, something white and blurry, and a pinkish and brown blur on top of that.

The glasses would have to stay.

She grabbed her bag off of the bed, slung it over her shoulder, and went downstairs. She reached the front door just as the doorbell rang.

She peered through the peep-hole, and was surprised to see no-one there. And then the doorbell rang again, making Sophie jump back in surprise. She looked through the peep-hole again, but still saw no-one outside.

Making sure the chain was on, she eased the door open to see if she could find out what was going on.

"Sophie! It's me, Emily...let me in!"

Breathing a sigh of either relief of exasperation - it was hard to tell which - Sophie unchained the door and opened it wide. There stood Emily, all four and a half feet of her, beaming from ear to ear. Sophie, who was over a foot taller than Emily, smiled back.

"Emily, why are we smiling like psychos?"

"I'm smiling because I'm excited. You're the one smiling like a psycho."

Sophie's face dropped. "Why are you excited?"

"Because it's Tuesday, and that means we're starting the new play tonight! That's where we're going!"

"That's where *I'm* going. I don't remember you

mentioning you were going along this time, especially after what you said to that Lucy last time. Anyway, you nearly missed me."

"Well I know I didn't make a formal declaration or anything, but I rang Jim, and he said there's a part for me. And you know, you only live just down the street from me, and we've been best friends for *ages*. It makes more sense to go together."

"Uh huh...we're friends, sure. But it's not like we're going in a car or anything..."

"No, but we can chat while we walk! We hardly ever talk these days!"

"Yeah, I know..."

"And since the thing with Lucy and Chris, the door is open for you! She turned him down so he's still available!"

"What's that supposed to mean? What even makes you think I'm interested?"

"Oh, nothing. Everything. You know you like him."

"I like ponies too, but I'm not about to ask on out on a date."

"Ha! You admit it then!"

"Admit what?"

"You said, 'I like ponies *too*'! Like, as well as Chris! I win!"

"Yeah, whatever, you win. Just let me get my jacket, then we can go."

"Yay!"

"Stop it. *Now*. I swear, if you embarrass me, I'll tell Chris you changed your mind."

***

The Bentley Hill Players had been around for almost 70 years, and during that time had attracted the finest talent that Bentley Hill had to offer. To be fair, Bentley Hill was a very small place, nestled in the hills of Derbyshire. It wasn't even a town. It existed as the footnote to the town of Blackworth, only to be mentioned in passing, and often avoided at all costs. Where Blackworth held pride of place as the-town-on-top-of-the-hill, Bentley Hill was, in spite of the name, actually at the *bottom* of the hill. This made the whole place susceptible to flooding, and also ensured that the main road through Bentley Hill was treated as a race track by everyone who had driven all the way down from Blackworth on their way to somewhere more exciting Bentley Hill.

But Bentley Hill was the kind of place that once you moved too, you didn't move away again. The locals wouldn't let you. They'd either make you feel very welcome, or they'd steal the wheels of your car. Either way, you weren't leaving.

On the side of Bentley Hill furthest away from Blackworth (which only made a difference of about 800 yards) was a small pub, *The Hill Tavern*. This in itself was a bit of a joke, as The Hill Tavern was actually at the lowest point in Bentley Hill. If anything, it was in it's own little valley, as far removed from being on a hill as possible.

The Tavern was on the corner of Main Road and Converse Road. The Tavern held two great benefits for the Players; first, the landlord was a good friend of Jim, and let them use the upstairs room for free every now and then, and second, the hall where the Players performed was only a hundred yards or so down Converse Road. This meant that if they rehearsed at the hall, the Tavern was just a short walk away. But most things were only a short walk away in Bentley Hill.

On this particular late summer evening, Jim

and Anne were the first to arrive, which was not uncommon or unexpected as Jim was known to enjoy a pint or two. Jim sat at the head of the long table in the upstairs room, nursing a pint, whilst Anne looked at her glass of wine, wishing it were twice as large. And possibly filled with something stronger.

Next to arrive was Lillian Lovelace, the elder stateswoman of the Bentley Hill Players. She was 90 if she was a day, but still full of life, with a head full of hair and all her own teeth, as she was apt to remind anyone who would listen. In her head, she was still 18, and often acted like she was younger than that. She came up the stairs under her own power, carrying a pint in one hand and her extravagant hat in the other.

Sophie and Emily arrived next, both sitting down at the table with a glass of wine. Jim raised his eyebrows.

"Is she old enough for that?" he asked Sophie.

Emily looked hurt. "I'm 19, Mr Butler. How old do you think I am?"

"19, but only because you just said so. I'm not getting thrown out of here because of under-age drinkers."

"But you didn't serve me!"

"Doesn't matter. I'm a witness."

There was a loud bang, and everyone looked at the stairs.

"Oops."

It was Owen O'Donnell, a Players regular, standing there looking sheepish. At his feet lay a dark blue canvas bag with large brown handles. Holding a pint in his right hand, he picked the bag up - with a considerable amount of effort - with his left.

"Just brought a few things with me. Not to worry!"

A few years north of forty, Owen wore sweaters that looked like rejects from a Christmas shop - all year round. His curly black hair was beginning to grey around the temples, and his lazy eye never meant you knew if he was addressing you or the person next to you. Today's ensemble was completed by a pair of bottle green trousers and brown shoes, one of which was tied with a piece of green gardening string. Standing just a few inches taller than Emily, he gave the distinct impression of an alcoholic garden gnome who had just lost his fishing rod.

"What's in the bag today, Owen?", asked Lillian.

"Oh, just a few things I need. Notepad. Pens. Bottle of gin. Bowling ball. Clean pair of socks."

Before anyone could question Owen further, Harry and Chris arrived.

"Hey gang, the party people have arrived!" shouted Chris.

Harry looked unconvinced that he was a "party-person", whatever Chris considered a "party-person" to be. Greetings were exchanged all round, and Jim rose to speak.

"I think everyone is here now, so we'd best get started. Don't want to go on all night, do we? So, first things first. Our next production could well be our last...."

A chorus of "aww" and "oh no" erupted around him.

"No, no, it may have to be that way. The Bentley Hill Players have been around my entire life, but it looks like it could be the end of the road. My grandfather Eric Butler was one of the founding members, and performed with my own father, Frank, in *An Inspector Calls*. The Players are basically a family heirloom. But as with many heirlooms, the sentimental value often outweighs the monetary value. Fact is, we're nearly broke. We have to pay for costumes, scenery, and so on, but most of all, we have to pay to hire the hall from Tom McLean, and it's not cheap..."

A cough came from the stairs. As she stepped in to the room, Zoe McLean smiled, and raised her hand by way of acknowledgement.

"Don't mind me, carry on. Sorry I'm late. Dad dropped me off, but he didn't get in from work until late. Sorry. Carry on."

"Ah", said Jim. "I was just talking about the hall and your father..."

"I know. I heard. But he has to make his money somehow!"

"Granted, and I know that the hall is only a small concern for him, but it does take a large chunk out of our budget. But of course, that has nothing to do with you, so come in and join us. The more the merrier!"

"Hi Zoe!", said Chris. Harry elbowed him under the table.

"Hi Chris. Hope Harry didn't hurt you too much there."

Chris glared at Harry. Emily grinned at Sophie. Sophie stared in to her own lap.

"Anyone want a bit of gin?", asked Owen.

"No!", said Jim. "You *will* get us thrown out if you start pouring your own alcohol! Now listen up you lot, this is the important bit. Our next, and possibly final play, is a *spooktacular* comedy written by my late father. It's called *The Ghost Under The Stairs*, and we're aiming for a performance in late November or early December to try and get the Christmas-ghost-story vibe. It's the story of two sisters who inherit a fortune, one of whom tries to steal it from the other, and the ghost who saves the day. Our biggest problem is going to be working out how to perform as the ghost. I don't think a sheet with holes cut in it will be good enough."

Harry jumped in. "We could try and do it like they did in Victorian theatre. You know, with a light and an angled piece of glass, so it's kind of like a mirror, but transparent."

"Sounds good, but sheets of glass might be dangerous with Owen around. And it could be expensive. Remember, we're on a budget here!"

"What about ticket sales?", asked Chris. "Won't we take enough from them to splash out a bit?"

"We can always hope, but we never seem to get a packed house. And of course, Tom will still want his pound of flesh..."

Zoe coughed.

"...which of course he's entitled to as it such a beautiful hall. Isn't that right, Zoe?"

"Absolutely. I wasn't coughing because of what you said, you know, I just need a drink."

"What can I get for you?", asked Chris. Harry elbowed him again, causing him to cough.

"I'll just have a cola, please, Chris. You could probably do with one yourself, what with that cough you have there."

"Sophie needs a drink too", said Emily.

"Shut up Emily..."

"No probs. What did you want, Sophie?", asked Chris.

"White wine, please," said Sophie, staring at what had suddenly become a very interesting spot on the table.

"Anyone else?"

Everyone put in their requests, and Chris made his way down the stairs to order at the bar.

Sophie kicked Emily under the table. Emily smiled and gave her a 'thumbs-up' sign.

Chapter 4

The following evening, Dave Sweet sat alone in his sparse living room. Two armchairs, a small table, and a TV - what more could he need? The room was illuminated by light from the setting sun, and a small orange candle on the table.

Dave sat and stared at the candle, deep in thought, imagining everything his life could have been. He could have been an entrepreneur. He could have been a millionaire. He could have been a professional football player. He could have been a rock star. Fantasies of how his life could have been whirled through his mind, but in the end, he could only focus on where he had ended up.

Cleaning up after everyone else.

His mind returned to the events of Friday night, when he'd heard the voice again. It was becoming more and more regular. At first, it had been once a month, very faint, and just saying, "Look!"

Now it was every other time he went to the

hall. Now it was loud. Now it was telling him to look in the toilet, and he did *not* like that. Not one bit. Especially after the youth club had been in, because they never seemed to know how to flush the toilet. It may be old fashioned, but it's quite straightforward - just give the chain a good yank, and off you go.

A knock at the door snapped Dave back to reality.

"Go away. I paid it last week!"

There was a muffled thud, and the letterbox popped open.

"Very good! I like to know you keep up with your payments. Let me in, the gin is getting warm!"

"Owen! Hang on a mo!"

Dave threw back all four bolts on the door, and unfastened the two key-operated locks. The door swung open, and there stood Owen, blue canvas bag at his feet.

"Could die of cold out here! I'm coming in!"

"Cold? I thought you said the gin was getting *warm*.."

Owen picked up his bag and barged in, plopped himself down in an armchair, and dropped his bag with another loud thud at his feet.

"Come on then. Let's be having you!" he said.

Dave closed the door and locked just one of the two locks, feeling safer with Owen as company. He sat in the other armchair, which was uncomfortably cold, as Owen had taken the one Dave had previously occupied. Owen produced a pair of paper party hats from his bag, along with two plastic cups and a bottle of gin.

"Drink, fella?"

"Don't mind if I do."

As Owen poured, he looked up at Dave, expertly stopping before either of the cups overflowed.

"I suppose you've heard we'll be back at the hall soon?"

"I have indeed. Something else to clean up after."

"Hey, we don't make a mess!"

"No, but the audience does."

"Well, the way things are, there might not even *be* an audience. We might not make it that far. Money's tight right now, and hiring the hall isn't cheap."

"No, but McLean is! Haw haw!"

"Yeah, we were nearly caught out like that the other night. You'll never guess who was at the meeting...only his daughter! And she showed up half way through. But I reckon she was stood on the stairs listening in before that. She's a piece of work, that one."

"She's the blonde, ain't she?"

"That's the one."

"Hmm. She always seems like she's up to something. You're probably right. She'll have gone straight back to daddy to file her report."

"Well, I'm not too worried. McLean will be happy as long as he gets his money. And when I say happy, I mean, *no worse than usual*. But anyway, I wanted to talk to you about *The Ghost Under The Stairs*."

"No way! You've heard it too?"

"....heard what?"

"The ghost under the stairs!"

"Well no, not yet. We haven't had a read-through yet. But it looks OK."

"It looks OK? You've *seen* it! I've only heard it!"

"Seen what?"

"The ghost under the stairs!"

Owen took a swig of his gin. Dave thought Owen might be staring at him, but with the lazy eye, you could never be sure. Owen placed his cup on the table.

"You've heard *The Ghost Under the Stairs*. Is that what you're saying?"

"Yes."

"And when did you hear it?"

"Friday was the last time."

"And where did you hear it?"

"At the hall! I was on my own, getting ready to leave, but if you don't get out fast enough, it's there. Every time now. Used to be once a month."

Owen took another swig from his cup, draining it. He refilled it, took another swig, and scratched his chin.

"I think we may be talking at cross-purposes. I'm hoping we aren't, but I think we are. On Friday, what *exactly* did you hear?"

"The ghost under the stairs. Well, actually, I think it's more under the stage. But then it comes out, and there's a loud noise, and then it talks to me."

"Right, that's unfortunately what I thought you were trying to say. I was actually talking about the play called *The Ghost Under The Stairs*. But you were talking about an actual supernatural entity."

"Yes. Oh, *I see*. Oh. That's quite funny really, isn't it?"

"Well, no, not really. Not if there's an actual ghost! What does it say to you?"

"*Look in the toilet!*"

"What for? Have you written the message on toilet paper?"

"No, no, that's what it says. *Look in the toilet*. It used to just say 'look', but it seems much more specific now."

"And have you looked in the toilet?"

"No."

"Why not?"

"Would *you* look in a toilet at that place just because a ghost told you to?"

***

"Ant so, ant, ant, ant so, I says to 'im, you can put yer own foot in it!"

It was nearly midnight, and Owen's alcohol had been used up, along with several cans of beer that Dave had in the fridge. The night had reached the stage where stories of previous exploits were told, with all thoughts of supernatural entities long since forgotten.

"But Dave, surely the lady mayoress would have had to move the mice first? Thass juss cruel, that is."

"I know, right? But the coach driver couldn't put his hat back on at all!"

"And where did you say they found his underpants?"

"On the weathervane! I mean, I ask you!"

Dave's wristwatch staring beeping. Owen checked his own watch to see what the time was.

"Aw no, s'midnight. Time to go home. I haff to be up early, as I am meeting with a lady friend of mine to discuss some business."

"Who is that then?"

"That's for me to know and you to see on the

evening news!"

"Your sister then?"

"Yeah, taking her shopping. Right, I'm off!"

Owen took three attempts to rise from his chair, and promptly sat down again when he tried to pick up his bag. Then, in one graceful movement, he managed to do both things at once, and staggered towards the front door. Dave followed him, unlocked the door, and swung it open. He stood to attention and saluted Owen.

"Your carriage awaits, m'lady."

"Thank you Jeeves. We must do this again!"

Dave could still hear Owen laughing his way down the street even after he'd done up all the locks and bolts, and had returned to his chair by the table.

***

Owen O'Donnell believed in magic. He believed in fairies too. He believed in dragons, monsters, zombies and vampires, but was not too sure about ghosts. Everything else, he didn't need to see to believe. But ghosts were special. Owen needed to see a ghost to believe that ghosts existed.

With this in mind, instead of going home as he originally intended, he ended up going in the opposite direction, towards the hall. Under normal circumstances he would have been there in ten minutes, but the gin had made his knees feel heavy, and it took him nearly three quarters of an hour.

He stood at the end of the path to the front door of the hall, hands on hips, bag at feet. He looked up to the roof, and down to the ground. Nothing seemed out of the ordinary.

And then he heard it.

"......you....."

Owen looked around. There was no-one in sight, and the street was deathly quiet.

".....yes, you...."

It was coming from the hall. Owen picked up his bag and walked up the path to the door.

"....better....can hear me now...drunk..."

"Hello?"

"...hello?"

"Can you speak up?"

"....speak up?"

"Hah. It's just an echo. Dave is an alcoholic, there is no ghost, and that's all there is to it."

"...in the toilet."

"What?!"

"...look in the toilet. Hello? Is this thing on? CAN YOU HEAR ME NOW? I SAID, *LOOK IN THE TOILET*!"

Owen ran as fast as he could back down the path and towards home. He suddenly stopped, turned on his heel, and ran back to the hall. He picked up his bag, and ran (considerably more slowly) towards home again.

"....will somebody look in the damn toilet, *please*?"

THE GHOST UNDER THE STAIRS

Chapter 5

Jim and Anne Butler lived a small bungalow half way up the hill to Blackworth. There was much debate as to whether their street was part of Blackworth, or part of Bentley Hill. Jim himself believed he lived in Bentley Hill, but Anne felt that living in Blackworth was slightly more classy. As far as it went with any maps the local council had drawn, the front room was in Bentley Hill but the conservatory was in Blackworth. This is the main reason that maps showing boundaries should be more accurate than they usually are, but the same council controlled both areas, so it wasn't a major problem.

The conservatory was the focus of activity this evening, along with the kitchen. Tonight was the night of the first read-through of *The Ghost Under the Stairs* by the Bentley Hill Players, and the Butler's conservatory was the ideal location to hold this event. Quieter than the Tavern, cheaper than the hall, and with plenty of snacks available from the aforementioned kitchen, it was perfect.

A large dining table was set up in the centre of the conservatory, and the view of Jim and Anne's beautiful garden was exceptional.

Everyone except Owen and Zoe arrived between 7 and quarter past. Jim had let everyone know the reading would start at twenty past, banking on everyone remembering this time. Something o'clock, quarter past or half past were too easy to forget. Everyone had things starting at those times. No-one seemed to do twenty past, so twenty past it was.

Anne came out of the kitchen carrying a tray with steaming hot drinks.

"Is Owen still not here? He's normally first at the door when he knows there's free food!"

"Maybe he's gone bowling," said Sophie. "Why does he carry that ball everywhere?"

"Just so he's ready," said Jim. "He likes to be prepared. Prepared for what, mind, I don't know. Always has a bottle of booze with him too. Maybe he's had a spot too much this afternoon and is sleeping it off!"

The doorbell rang.

"Hah, speak of the devil. That'll be the little fella right now!"

Jim rose from his seat and walked through the bungalow to the front door. He opened it with a large smile on his face.

"Welcome friend, I hope you've sobered up enough to...oh!"

There stood Zoe McLean, with her father just behind her. Tom McLean was not a tall man, but was wide and somehow physically imposing. He oozed alpha-maleness with his thick beard, closely cropped hair, and perfectly fitting suit.

"Good evening, James. I hope Zoe will be safe here at your AA meeting. What time are you finishing?"

"Er, hi, Tom. I wasn't expecting you..."

"No, clearly not."

"We should be done by half nine."

"Righto. I'll be back then, Zoe. And if he tries to ply you with drink, you have my permission to kick him in the shins. Always a pleasure, James."

Tom flashed a very clearly false smile through his beard, turned away, and walked back towards his Mercedes.

"Yes, always a pleasure, Tom. I hope your hair falls out," he added under his breath.

Zoe coughed.

"Sorry, Zoe."

***

"I think we should start without him. It's quarter to eight now, so I don't think he's coming."

Emily was concerned that she would be late home. Since her father had left, looking after her mother had become almost a full time job. Emily's mother was only in her late thirties, but after her husband had gone out for a walk one day and not come back, she'd just about given up on life. If Emily was late back, it would be as if the world had ended, and Emily could do without that kind of drama tonight. The only drama she was interested in was written in the script in front of her.

"Right," said Jim. "Let's crack on then. You all know which parts you're reading for, and I'll read in Owen's lines."

"That is going to get confusing," said Christopher.

Zoe and Sophie both smiled at him, one more kindly than the other.

"Don't you worry your pretty little head. You'll be OK," said Zoe.

"Hey, be nice," said Sophie. "He's not just a pretty head. I mean, sorry, Chris. I mean, er..."

"It's fine, Sophie. I know what you meant," said Christopher. He elbowed Harry. "Zoe thinks I'm pretty!" he whispered.

"Settle down!" said Jim. "Right, it's a dark stormy night, so we'll have a recording of a thunderstorm playing to start off with. Couple of flashing lights matched up to it, the usual. Enter stage right Miss Priscilla. That's you, Zoe."

"Oh lawks, what to do! Father is so ill, and may never recover..."

"...if only..." muttered Anne.

"...and the night is so full of strange noises. A creak here, a rattle there, the sound of a scream in the distance!"

There was the sound of a scream in the distance.

"The hell was that?" said Harry.

"Well, I don't want to be too much of a smarty-pants, but it sounded like a scream in the distance," said Christopher.

"Don't worry, we don't think you're smart," said Zoe.

There was a loud creaking noise coming from the side of the bungalow now. Suddenly, there was another scream in the distance, a loud cracking noise, and a thud followed by a low rumbling noise. Everyone looked out of the conservatory in the direction of the noise. A bowling ball slowly rolled round the side of the house, and came to a stop, along with the rumbling, on the lawn.

"It's Owen!" said Jim.

He jumped to his feet, unlocked the conservatory doors, and went to investigate.

***

"Owen lad, are you all right there?"

Owen was on his hands and knees around the side of the bungalow, with a large branch wedged between his legs. His bag was still held by a single handle in his right hand, but he'd lost his grip on the other handle. The contents of his bag had started to spill out, most noticeably with the bowling ball.

"I'm fine, don't worry. Didn't want to cause any bother. Had to sneak round, being followed and all that."

Owen looked up and grinned. He always seemed to have too many teeth for his mouth, perfectly straight, all yellow and brown.

"What do you mean, *being followed*?" asked Jim.

"Made a bit of an error of judgment. Stuck my nose in where it didn't belong. Clean pants time. Did you know spirits can follow you?"

"You mean you've had too much gin?"

"Yes. That as well. Went to the hall, ghost under the stairs, woooOOOOoOOOO. Toilets. Probably following me. Had to sneak in the back way so you and the ghost didn't notice. That tree isn't as strong as it looks."

"You could have knocked on the door, Owen..."

"Yes, but I would have disturbed your read-through then, because I'm late. *And* being followed by a ghost."

"You've disturbed it anyway, you idiot. Come

on inside."

***

While Owen went to the bathroom to clean himself up (nobody thought a read through with a man covered in tree bark, leaves, and mud was a good idea), the others tried to make sense of what was going on.

"It's quite simple," said Jim in a hushed voice. "He's drunk as the proverbial."

"He actually seems less drunk than usual," said Sophie.

"How can you tell?" asked Harry.

"He looks less cross-eyed."

"That's a medical condition," said Jim. "If he *is* less cross-eyed, it's because he banged his head when he fell out that tree. And I think he did bang his head, because he reckons he's being followed by a ghost."

"A ghost?"

"Yes Sophie, a ghost. He even did a *wooOOOoo* as if to prove it."

"Did you hear that?" said Owen, as he came back in to the conservatory. "It's here!"

"Owen, did you bang your head when you fell out the tree?"

"No, I did not, Jim. And I get the feeling you don't believe me."

"Well, it is a bit far-fetched..."

"Let me tell you, I went to see Dave the janitor the other night. He told me that if you are in the hall around midnight, you can hear it. It's a real ghost under the stairs! Or was it the stage? One of them. So I had a stiff drink to settle my nerves, and..."

"Just the one?"

"Yes. One. Ish. One bottle. Of drink. Anyway, that's not the point. I went down to the hall, and I heard it. Screaming it was, screaming. And it threatened me."

"Let me get this straight," said Jim. "You got drunk, went down the hall, and heard voices?"

"Spot on, Jimmy Jam Jimbo. Except, I wasn't drunk."

"How? You normally are!"

"Well, not *that* drunk. I heard it rise from the

grave, and it threatened me..."

"Rise from the grave? Where is there a grave at the hall?"

"Well, it's a figure of speech. It must have risen from the stage, that sounds a bit like *grave*. And it threatened me..."

"So you said."

"It did! It said I would have bad luck, and it would put me in the toilet!"

Everyone sat and looked at Owen. Emily broke the silence.

"You heard a ghost say it would put you in the toilet?"

"Yes, my friends, I did."

"In the toilet."

"Yes."

"The toilet."

"Yes."

"How would you even fit in a toilet?"

"The spirit world has mysterious ways, woooOOOOOOooooOOOO!"

"Right, Owen," said Jim. "Settle down. Are we

going to get on with this reading or not?"

"You don't believe me!"

"Does it really matter if I believe you or not?"

"Well....no. Proceed. But if I end up in a toilet, I'm going to blame you, Jim Butler. You mark my words. One flush and it would all be over."

***

"....and it all worked out in the end because of the ghost. The ghost from under the stairs!"

"Excellent, Sophie! That was actually rather good for a first read-through. What do the rest of you think?" asked Jim.

"Yeah, enjoyed that," said Sophie.

"I still think Priscilla should have got the fortune, not her sister. Sophie would just spend it on sweaters," said Zoe.

"Shut up Zoe," said Emily. "Sophie would not buy sweaters. Anyway, it's Sophie's character, not Sophie herself!"

"I don't like ghosts," said Owen.

"Ooh, yes please!" said Lillian. "I love toast,

me!"

"I thought you were great, Zoe," said Christopher.

"You were all great," said Harry, glaring at Christopher.

"Anyone want another cuppa, or are you all going to rush off now?" asked Anne.

"I'd best get going," said Harry. "You coming too?" he asked Christopher.

"Yeah, I'd better."

"I'm off too," said Sophie.

"I'll come with - it's dark now," said Emily.

"I can manage a cuppa", said Lillian.

"And I'll have one if there's a chance of a little drop in it, if you know what I mean..." said Owen.

"I think my dad's here," said Zoe. "I just saw some headlights stop at the end of the drive."

"Let me walk you to the door," said Christopher.

"It's not like she's flamin' disabled," muttered Sophie under her breath.

"Not deaf either," whispered Zoe with a wink.

***

"I insist Lillian, it's gone eleven, you are not walking home. Come on."

Independent to the end, Lillian had expressed her wish to Jim to walk home and enjoy the "bracing night breeze". Jim would have none of it, nor did he feel it was safe to let Owen walk home either. He bundled them both in to his car, waved *goodbye* to Anne, and drove them both home.

He dropped Owen off first as he lived nearest, and then he took Lillian to her ground floor flat. Ever the gentleman, he walked her up to her front door, and made sure she was safely inside before returning to the car.

Jim sighed deeply.

"Ridiculous. As if the hall is haunted."

He started the engine, and set off towards the hall.

***

11:59

The green digital readout on the dashboard showed there were just sixty seconds remaining until midnight. Jim opened the car door, and stepped out in to the cold night air. He was surprised to note that he could actually see his breath.

Jim strolled up the path to the front door of the hall. *That sign needs repainting*, he thought. ***Bent ill mun ty all*** *doesn't sound right*.

He cupped his hand over his eyes and peered through the glass portion of the door. Pitch black, nothing to see.

"Silly bugger. Too much gin as always."

Jim turned and walked back to his car....

...and then he heard it. A low, soft, droning sound. Like a sleepy bee that was just waking up. It grew louder and louder, and then there was an almighty bang.

"THE TOILET! THE BLASTED TOILET! HOW HARD IS IT TO GO TO THE TOILET? GET IN THERE! NOW!"

Chapter 6

By Wednesday evening, Jim had decided that he'd imagined the whole event. In any case, he had more things to worry about than the probably-imaginary spook in Bentley Community Hall.

For starters, Tom had increased the rates for hiring the hall. With the budget as tight as it was, any extra expense had the potential to kill the entire production, but this was something Jim didn't want to even consider.

Worse still, Owen has gone from worrying that a ghost may be following him to being downright paranoid. He'd only left his house twice since the last meeting, both times to go to the off-licence. Jim had spoken to him on the phone, and had a heck of a time convincing him to come out for a second read-through.

Emily, playing the love interest for Harry's character, had come down with a severe cold. She was clearly unable to attend the second read-through, as her very presence could cause half the cast to catch it too. Perhaps more importantly, her voice would have been most off-putting. Imagine Barry White gargling razor blades. Deeper. Deeper. Nearly there. That's it.

Several discussions between Jim and Harry regarding the ghostly special effects had yielded no results. Harry had been the main force behind scenery and effect design for several years now, and if he couldn't come up with a way to do something, there probably wasn't a way to do it. The best that Harry and Jim had come up with so far involved a wireless microphone, a sheet painted with glow-in-the-dark-paint, and a system of pulleys. As Jim would be portraying the ghost (and therefore most likely to be under the sheet), "a system of pulleys" was not a phrase he enjoyed hearing. Especially at his time of life.

As usual, the read-through was due to start at 7:20PM. Everyone was on time for once, even Owen. At least, everyone thought it was Owen, but it was hard to tell. The body was the right height, and wore the right kind of sweater and trousers, but the rest was open to debate. Maybe-it's-Owen wore large green gardening boots, a pair of oven gloves, and a knitted balaclava with eyeholes covered by a pair of sunglasses. No actually identifiable human part was visible.

Anne had let Maybe-it's-Owen in whilst Jim was in the bathroom. Maybe-it's-Owen had settled in at the table by the time Jim returned. Jim stepped in to the conservatory, and stopped dead in his tracks.

"What on earth are you wearing, Owen?"

"Suffa trection, Chim."

"What?"

"Suffa trection. Serda gerst cont gemme."

"So the ghost can't get you?"

"Rart. Furrie patrected."

"Oh I get it, *it's for protection*. How do the oven gloves protect you?"

"Con seema skin. Con gemme."

"Yeah, I don't think that's how it works. Anyway, this whole thing is hooey. There's no chance that hall is haunted. Ah, here's Anne with the tea. Would you like a biscuit to go with yours, Owen?"

"Mmm, hass untly wood."

"Here you go," said Jim, holding out a plate to Owen.

"Huggah!"

"Problem?"

Owen took off his oven gloves, and rolled the bottom of the balaclava up over his nose.

"I suppose I can risk a bit of skin. I'm indoors after all. Any whiskey for the tea?"

***

"....and it all worked out in the end because of the ghost. The ghost from under the stairs!"

"Where?!"

"It's fine Owen," said Jim. "It's still the play.

"Oh, good."

"Right, anyone staying for a bit, or are you all off again?"

There seemed to be a dividing line in the Bentley Hill Players, where those under 40 would leave almost immediately, and those over 40 would hang around for chat, enjoying the company, and possibly the alcohol. Tonight was no exception, apart from Zoe having to wait for her dad to pick her up. He was uncharacteristically late.

"You sure you're going to wait, Zoe? Me and Harry can walk you home..."

"Chris, you're going to have to walk her on your own. I need to get home myself, get ready for work in the morning."

"No problemo, amigo. Zoe?"

Christopher offered his hand. Zoe looked at it, and then back at his face.

"Sorry, Chris, I've got to wait for my dad. He'll go mad if I walk home in the dark."

"CHRIS!" shouted Sophie from down by the road. "YOU CAN WALK WITH ME IF YOU WANT!"

"No, it's OK," said Chris.

Sophie rolled her eyes and shrugged, and stomped off up the street.

"Missed your chance there, loverboy," said Zoe.

"Uh huh. Guess I did. HOLD UP HARRY! See ya later, Zoe."

Christopher raced after Harry. Jim watched him through the front window.

"I'm sure the boy means well, but he's such an

idiot sometimes. You're welcome to stay as long as it takes, Zoe, no worries there. I'm sure your dad..."

At just that moment, Tom McLean's car pulled up outside. Before Zoe could get out the front door, Tom had leapt from the car and was on his way up the path.

"Hey, dad. What's up?"

"I've come to have a word with Jim. *JAMES*?"

"Hi Tom, what can I do for you?"

"Well, not much, as it happens. I've come to let you know that I'm selling the hall. There's a couple of developers interested in the land, and it will probably fetch about two fifty at auction. I've just got off the phone with my team, and it's going to the auction second weekend in December, so you'll just have time for your little play, and then, if you'll excuse the pun, it's curtains."

"Developers? You mean they're going to demolish it, don't you?"

"Yep. And probably build a swanky new set of apartments. Unless I get an offer above 250 before then of course, in which case I'd sell immediately, which would be unfortunate as your little play would have to be cancelled. Already have the solicitor on a retainer! Sorry James, you know how it is, business and all that."

"Yes, I know...but...what will we do then?"

"Not really my concern, chap, is it? As it stands, I'm making virtually nothing from the place as it is. In fact, it's costing money every month. That's why the costs for hiring have had to go up. Electric bills, water bills, the council wanting a cut and so on. A cool quarter mil would go a long way towards easing my pain, don't you think? Considering I paid less than half that for it in the first place! Right, nice chatting to you, but I don't have all night to waste. C'mon Zoe, poppet, let's go. Ciao!"

Tom turned and strode quickly back towards his parked car. Zoe looked at Jim, their faces a mirror image of shock.

"I...I...don't know what to say. I'm so sorry, Jim. I...I don't know. I'll talk to him, but I know when he makes his mind up, you're best to get out of his way..."

"Zoe love, it's not your fault. Don't worry we'll work it out. See you Friday?"

"Yes...if I'm still welcome?"

"Of course you are!"

Tom's window rolled down.

*"ZOE.....**POPPET**!"*

"You'd best go," said Jim.

"OK. See you Friday," said Zoe.

Jim watched Zoe get in the passenger door, and waved as the car drove off. He went back in the bungalow and closed the door behind him.

"What was all that about?" asked Lillian.

"Tom's selling the hall. This next performance might not be our last at all...we might already be finished."

Act II

Chapter 7

An emergency meeting of the Bentley Hill Players had never been called before. There had never been an emergency that required a meeting in the entire history of the Players, mostly because there are very few emergencies that are improved by holding a meeting. But this particular emergency - the impending doom of the Bentley Community Hall as a place to perform - was considered exceptional.

Everyone was at the Tavern early, including Zoe. She had thought it best to catch the bus to the meeting, rather than having her father bring her. Just the fact that she shared a surname with the man who was about to snatch the hall away was likely to cause enough friction with the rest of the Players.

"Whatever happens," said Jim, "we are in no position to purchase the hall. We hardly have enough money to rent it to put on a show! So everyone forget that idea before you even think of it."

"What if we all bought lottery tickets?" asked Chris.

Harry laughed. "I think it might be better if we all put the money to buy lottery tickets in a large pot..."

"...and used it to buy another round of drinks! *Great idea Harry*!", said Owen.

"But we might get lucky!" said Chris.

"We might not as well," said Jim. "All we can do is sell as many tickets as we can, and hope that the building is still standing when it's opening night."

"How many tickets would we need to sell?"

"Well, we can get about two hundred folk in there easily, by which I mean they'll fit. It's not easy to sell tickets to two hundred people. If we did, and the tickets were a fiver each, that would be a thousand quid a night. Over the three nights, that's obviously three thousand, and Tom wants a thousand to rent the place. That's for three nights, and use of the stage prior to that, for sorting out the scenery and so on. So best case, we come out with two grand, less costs. Our costs will be in the region of five hundred, what with costumes, scenery, ticket printing, and whatever we can do for promoting the show, like posters."

"That's good then! We'd make fifteen hundred quid!"

"You're forgetting one important factor there, Chris. These days, we never sell out. Ever. If we're half full, it's a busy night!"

"So why not just double the ticket price to a tenner? Half as many people, double the price, same result!"

"Because if we do, even less people will turn up. Five quid is five quid, but when you start looking at a ten pound note you start to imagine all the fish suppers you could buy with it instead!"

"Really?" said Harry. "If you go up to Blackworth you'll get about one and a half fish suppers for a tenner. They're not so cheap any more!"

"I could set up a kissing booth," said Lillian.

Everyone immediately stopped what they were doing. It took a moment for Jim to regain his wits.

"Why would you do that?" asked Jim.

"To sell tickets, of course!"

"I don't think that's how kissing booths work..."

"No, no, hear an old lady out. I set up the booth on the Blackworth market, and everyone who pays for a smooch gets a free ticket. And I'd charge six pounds for a kiss, so we'd be making extra!"

"I don't know where to start. Assuming it worked, how many people do you think would actually turn up? I mean, the money's fine, but we don't want to be performing to an empty room, do we? The point of performing is so people see it!"

"I would write *don't forget* on the tickets."

"OK, let's go back a step here. Suppose no-one actually pays you for a kiss..."

"Well that's very unlikely. I was Miss Blackworth Fields in 1964!"

"Uh huh. And half a century ago, we didn't have laptops, smartphones, colour TV, and the Beatles were all still alive..."

"...and there's still a lot of life left in me!" said Lillian, giving Jim a wink.

Jim shook his head in exasperation. "Any other ideas?"

"Zoe could do it!", said Chris.

"Do what?"

"The kissing booth!"

"*What*?" said Zoe.

Harry sighed. "I think what Chris is saying, is that Zoe might do better in a kissing booth situation than Lillian as she is...she's....she has *broader appeal* than Lillian."

"I think what Harry is trying to say", said Emily, giggling, "is that Chris has the hots for Zoe, and he'd spend a fortune at a kissing booth if she was in it."

"I would *not*!" said Chris.

"Oh, thank you very much. What's *that* supposed to mean?" asked Zoe.

"Stop everyone. I could do it. That will stop the arguing," said Sophie.

"**WE ARE NOT HAVING A KISSING BOOTH!**" yelled Jim. "We need to sell tickets, not kisses!"

"Sex sells, sweetie," said Lillian.

"What kind of kissing booth are you running, Lil?" said Jim. "We are not doing a kissing booth -

or a sex booth - no matter what. If I go to the market on Saturday and find *any one* of you selling kisses or sex or anything, there's going to be trouble."

"Selling sex?" said Harry. "Are you selling it by weight? I'll have a couple of ounces, please."

"Leave it, Harry. We're not doing it."

"I could cut up my net curtains and do the Dance of the Seven Veils!", said Lillian.

"Are we having another round?" said Owen. "I think I need another drink..."

***

"So maybe Lillian wasn't too far off with the kissing booth. What we need to do, is raise funds *and* sell tickets. The more money we have, the better scenery and costumes we'll have, and the more likely that people will enjoy it and tell their friends. More people, more money, full house, job done."

"But Jim, what can we do?" asked Harry. "Amateur theatre is so far off most people's radar these days. How can we do something that will get people interested?"

"I have an idea!", said Chris."

"No, you don't. She won't kiss you even if you pay her now."

"No, not that. And she might. You might, mightn't you, Zoe?"

Before Zoe could answer, Sophie interrupted. "I don't think that's important. What's the idea, Chris?"

"Well, I think it *might* be important. Anyway, we need to build interest by being *interesting*. Nobody cares about a bunch of amateurs in a creaky old hall, but everyone cares about...I don't know...X Factor? The only difference is that X Factor has been marketed to people, and they're interested in it."

"And it's on TV," said Sophie.

"I was on telly once," said Lillian.

Chris ignored her, and carried on, "Yeah, but it's not on TV to start with. They do the visiting cities thing first."

"Which they film and put on the telly."

"No, wait," said Jim. "He might be right. Before they hold the auditions, they advertise them. I'm pretty sure they mention it on the TV at some stage, but there must be adverts in local papers, and posters, and stuff like that. But there again, we've tried that before and it hasn't made that much difference."

"That's because we haven't made a big enough splash. We need to be *like* the telly. We need to get in front of people and make a noise about what we are doing."

"I can make some tremendous noises," said Owen. "Have any of you been to that new Indian take-away on the Bentley View estate? All the houses look the same, but the curry is very different. Couldn't stop my bottom from singing afterwards."

"No," said Jim, "that's not the kind of noise we need to make. That would turn people away rather than bring them in."

"What we need to do," said Chris, slowly rising from his chair, "is let people know we are here. That we've been here for many years, and we aren't going away soon. We were born to act, and act we will."

Owen began to hum *Land of Hope and Glory* under his breath.

"We will meet them, in the market place. We will meet them, in the town. We will tell them, what we are about and what we will do, and in the end, you will see that never have so many tickets been sold by so few, to people in the market. Or something like that. We need to get dressed up and do a few skits in the town on market day. Shut *up,* Owen!"

"Sorry chap. *What* did you say we needed to do in the town?"

"Skits. Little scenes, show off our abilities. You wouldn't buy a car or a house without seeing it, so why would you come to a show without knowing what to expect."

"That's a pretty good idea, lad," said Jim. "A few snippets of *The Ghost* and we could get them hooked. It's like a drug!"

"Where?" said Owen, his eyes darting around rapidly.

"We should hand out flyers, too," said Harry. "I know a guy at work who'd knock us something up. Could probably get a few hundred for a tenner."

"Good stuff," said Jim. "I think this just might work. All we have to do is hope that the hall is still there after all this!"

Everyone turned to look at Zoe.

"*What*?" she said.

***

Harry and Chris left the Tavern at half past ten. It had started raining while they were in there, but it was only a short walk home, so they made the best of it. And walked quickly.

"So what do you reckon to all this about there being a ghost in the hall?" asked Harry.

"I don't know. I mean, I'm not sure about ghosts in general. I've never seen one, but I know people who say they have, and I believe they saw...something. I know they aren't lying, but they might have been mistaken. But it's creepy all the same. Can you imagine being dead and still being stuck in Bentley Hill? Especially in the rain!"

Harry laughed. "Ah, it looks like we may have found the gate to hell. It's just off the M1, right near the turning to Blackworth. You're trapped...*FOREVER*! Muahaha!"

"Keep it up, you'll need all the practice you can get at being dramatic if we're doing this thing on the market!"

"It's you that needs practice, sunshine. You must conceal your true emotions, grasshopper. Not saying things like, *I'd spend a fortune on kissing Zoe*!"

"I didn't even say that! That was Sophie!"

"Whatever, you were thinking it, you dirty little dinky!"

"I don't even know what a dirty little dinky is, and I don't want you to show me either. Hey, look, there's someone in there!"

Without realising, they had reached the end of the path up to entrance of the Community Hall. The building was in darkness, but there was someone standing at one of the upstairs windows, illuminated by the street lamps.

"Is it Dave?"

"I don't think so. He'd have the lights on, wouldn't he?"

***

Owen had finished one too many drinks. No, wait. Owen had too many drinks - far too many.

He left the tavern waving to Harry and Chris, shouted something about a plum pudding to Lillian, and staggered off down the street, with his bag scraping on the ground beside him. Unfortunately, he wasn't so sure of where he lived any more, and headed in the wrong direction.

He fell through a hedge and landed in someone's back garden. A security light blinked on, and he stood shielding his eyes with his hand.

"Good evening ladies and gentles. Gentles. Gentry men. Men. Thank you."

The light went out.

"Everyone's a critic."

He staggered on, and fell through the hedge on the far side of the garden. He slowly rose to his feet, and decided he was in a field. Yes, definitely a farmer's field.

"I must go and congratulate the farmer on such a fantastic crop," he said, making his way to the farmhouse he thought he saw at the end of the field.

***

"OI! What are you up to in there?", yelled Harry.

Softly, a voice responded, "....hello?"

Harry and Chris looked at each other, eyes wide.

"H...h...hello?", said Harry.

"....hello? Marvellous place."

"Er...yes. Yes it is. Are you an actor?"

"...yes. Sometimes I am. Sometimes I drink too much and forget who I am, but I am indeed an actor. I have a message for you."

"Really? For us? What is it?"

"I've been out in the field, and it's great. Well done. Good work."

"Wow!" said Harry. "He's been out in the field, like touring! And now we're going out in the field, doing this performance on the market place. We have the support of the spirit world! THANK YOU!"

"No problem. Now, must dash, need to pee."

There was a creaking sound, followed by a loud bang.

Harry and Chris exchanged glances, turned

quickly, and started to run.

"WHO IS THAT YELLING OUT THERE? I'M NOT DUE UP YET! AND WHO ARE YOU? WHAT ARE YOU DOING? GET OUT OF THE BUSHES MAN, AND GET IN THE TOILET! YOU'RE GOING TO KILL THE GRASS! THE TOILET! FOR GOODNESS SAKE, THE TOILET! HOW HARD CAN IT BE?"

Chapter 8

The next few days saw the Bentley Hill Players meeting up every single night, rehearsing for their performance on the market place. Jim had selected two short scenes, one from near the start of the play and one from near the end. He hoped the scenes he had chosen would showcase the abilities of the cast, and invoke an emotional response from the captive audience on the market.

A decision was made to perform in regular street clothes, as work on the costumes hadn't even begun yet. *If you can interest them in jeans and a t-shirt*, Jim had thought, *you'll knock 'em out in full costume*. This pleased Anne no end, as it was normally down to her to make sure all the costumes were ready, and her sewing machine was in need of a service.

For Chris, the rehearsals were not going as well as he had hoped. His character, *Phabtasio Moncrieff*, was the boyfriend of *Ludmilla Conchetta*, played by Sophie. The problem was fundamental -

he couldn't pronounce any of the names.

"I mean, what the heck, these aren't even real names!"

"Look, come back to mine afterwards, and we'll go through it again," said Sophie.

"I guess I could. We need to get this spot on, or we're just gonna get laughed at."

"Well, it's been a good night tonight, apart from a few pronunciation issues," said Jim. "We've got a couple of days left, and then it's showtime. Good news is, I've checked the weather forecast, and it will be fine on Saturday. We just need to get our words out!"

"You coming then?" said Sophie.

"I guess so. Have you got any hair straighteners? I might try them on my tongue, see if it makes it any easier."

***

Sophie unlocked the door, and she and Chris went in to warm hallway of her parents house. Sophie stuck her head in to the living room.

"Hi mum, hi dad. I've just brought Chris home to practice his lines, is it OK if we use the kitchen? Yeah? Ta."

Sophie turned and walked to the kitchen. "C'mon, don't be shy. You *have* been here before!"

"I know, but not for ages. Hi, mister and missus Patterson!"

A muffled "Hi" came from the living room.

Sophie put the kettle on, and sat Chris down next to her at the kitchen table.

Chris cleared his throat, and looked deeply into Sophie's eyes. "My sweet, my love. For I will do anything for you, Ludilly. Sorry. Ludmil. Oh, for goodness sake..."

"Calm down Chris, deep breaths. Relax. Try again."

"My sweet, my love. For I will do anything for you, Clodmilla. Agh. Lomilolo. Nope, lost it."

"You know, you can really express the emotions when you try. I've seen you do it. It's just that you fall over the names, every single time, and then you lose the emotional connection. It breaks it for you, so it will break it for the audience. Can you say my name? I mean, my real name?"

"Well, yes. Sophie. Sophie. Sophie-bom-bophie. Easy."

"Try it with my name in the lines, then. Get a feel for it, then put the other names in later."

"OK, I guess it's worth a go. Ahem ahem ahem."

Chris looked down to the floor, and slowly raised his eyes to Sophie's, and gazed in to them intensely.

"My sweet, my love. For I will do anything for you, Sophie, and I will love you until the end of time. For Sophie, when I look in to your eyes, I see our future together. I see our lives entwined until the world is gone. And I will love you forever, and no-one will take me away from you, or you away from me."

Sophie mouth fell open, and a single tear fell from her eye.

"That's not in the script Sophie! How did you do that? I can't make myself cry..."

Sophie leaned forward and kissed Chris full on the lips. She slowly pulled away, holding on to his bottom lip until the last moment.

"That...that...that wasn't in the script either,

Sophie...wow...er....I'd better get going."

Chris got to his feet, his eyes never leaving Sophie's. He shook his head and blinked, and walked off towards the front door. He opened the door and stepped outside, and turned back to close the door behind him.

Sophie had followed him, and stood on the doorstep. He leaned in and gave her a quick kiss on the lips.

"I'll see you tomorrow, Sophie. Sleep tight."

Sophie watched him walk up the drive and in to the night.

***

"So I think it might be a good idea to use our real names on Saturday. And Sophie agrees."

"Well Chris, I think I'm going to have to agree too. If you're out there calling folk Pudkiller or whatever you came out with, they're going to think it's more of a comedy than it's meant to be. They should laugh at the jokes, not the actors. Let's do it! All in favour, say *aye*!"

It was unanimous, and the rehearsal went

perfectly. Chris had not spoken to Sophie since the previous evening, but as soon as he saw her that evening, he smiled broadly.

The only problem occurred when Chris reached his line about their love lasting forever, as he almost went to kiss Sophie, which was very much not in the script. Sophie realised what was happening, and had to bite her lip to prevent herself from laughing at the confused look on his face.

When the rehearsal was over, Sophie invited Chris back for a cup of coffee. Harry looked crestfallen when he found out that there would be no trip for pizza on this particular evening, but he couldn't put up any kind of argument when he saw the grin on Chris's face.

"Och, be careful laddy," he said, slipping in to that Scottish accent again. "Fur a wumman may nat be all that she sims! Not when she deprives me of pizza!"

"No, haven't got a clue what you just said. But anyway, I'm going for a cup of coffee, and her mam and dad are in the next bloody room. It's not a date, mate!"

"Aye, well ye can nevah be tae careful!"

"I thought you were in favour of me and Sophie! In any case, I'm going to stop you having red sweets, because they clearly send you hyper."

"Ye can tek ma freedom, but ye'll nevah tek mah sweeties! Awee with ye, ye wee whippersnapper!"

"Yeah, OK. See you tomorrow, mate!"

And so, Chris went home with Sophie, and they talked until midnight. And then Sophie's mum politely asked Chris if he had a home to go to. And he did, and so he went to it.

And that night, he dreamed of Sophie, and he dreamed of the hall. He dreamed of Sophie in the hall, and he dreamed of the shadow of a blue man. He dreamed of Zoe laughing and pointing, and he dreamed of Sophie tripping and falling. But most of all, he dreamed of the toilet. And he didn't know why.

Chapter 9

"Ohmygodohmygodohmygod"

"*EMILY*! Calm down!" yelled Harry. "You're going to pass out if you carry on like this."

"I'm sorry Harry, but there might be people I know out shopping today! What if they see me?"

"That's the entire idea of this, Emily - we want people to see us! Why did you think we were doing it?"

"I know but...people..."

A little way away, Chris was smiling - still - at Sophie.

"You know, that's getting a little creepy now. Can you look a little less happy?"

"Uh? Oh, sorry. Didn't realise I was doing it again."

"You weren't doing it again. You were *still* doing it."

"Sorry."

"It's OK. Just make sure you have the right expression on your face when you deliver your lines."

"Sorry."

"Stop saying sorry"

"Sorry. I mean, uh, sorry?"

Jim was pacing back and forth behind a fruit and veg stall. Anne was following him, two steps behind.

"It's all going to go wrong, I know it is. Someone will forget their lines, or trip and land in a watermelon."

"It'll be fine, Jim. They're not *all* idiots, you know!"

The vinyl tarpaulin covering the back of the stall slowly lifted, and Owen's face appeared beneath it.

"Jim! Anne! Shh! There's fruit in here!"

Jim stopped pacing. He looked stone-faced at Anne, who shrugged, and then looked back to Owen.

"Of course there's fruit, you numbskull. It's a fruit stall!"

"But it's freeeeee!"

"How is it free?"

"You just have to take it when that fella ain't looking!"

"GET OUT OF THERE! **NOW**! Anne, help me find Lillian, we need to get this thing started before that stall owner gives Owen a smack."

On the opposite side of the stall, Lillian was giving Zoe a few final words of advice.

"Now, when he gets on the horse, you just say *giddy up* and we'll be away."

"But Mrs Lovelace...there isn't a horse in this play."

"I know, but if there were, that's what you'd do."

"Are you feeling OK, Mrs Lovelace?"

"Never been better, Jim."

"I'm Zoe, Mrs Lovelace."

"And don't you forget it, Sophie!"

"Zoe..."

"No, no, Lillian. Lillian Lovelace. So pleased to meet you. Where's the horse?"

***

Owen shuffled between the shoppers, for once without his bag in his hand. The bag was behind the fruit stall, stuffed to the brim with bananas and kiwis. The bowling ball may still have been in there, but it may have been replaced by a large melon. It was hard to tell.

He looked to the sky, raised his hands above his head, and gave a maniacal laugh.

"Hahaha! For the inheritance shall soon all be ours, and we shall let not a single person stand in our way!"

A group of shoppers turned to look at him.

"For Zoe, tis true that your father has died and is not yet cold, but why should your inheritance be shared? A plan with poison and passion will shuffle the hand that fate has dealt, and we shall soon be away!"

"*You alright mate?*"

"Zoe! Give me the word and we shall begin!"

Zoe appeared from behind a stall selling mobile phone cases.

"Doctor Owen! The hand that fate has dealt must be shuffled, and you must begin now!"

"*Are you with* him, *love? He looks a bit mad to me...*"

Sophie walked from round the back of a sock stall.

"Sister! Who are you talking to? Why, tis the doctor! What is the problem?"

"Tis our father, sister. His time has come!"

"Nooo!", wailed Sophie. A woman with a pushchair ran quickly away from her.

Lillian pushed her way through the gathering crowd.

"I'm here! Where's me horse?"

Jim hissed from behind her, "Not yet, you fool!"

"I'm ready **now**!" she yelled in response. "Let's find a horse! Yeah!"

As she shouted, she raised an empty bottle over her head and gave it a shake, as if it were some kind of trophy.

"Oi!", shouted Owen. "That's where the gin went!"

He made a grab for the bottle, and tripped over his own feet. Harry and Chris ran to help him up, but Harry got caught on the head by Lillian swinging the bottle. He fell to his knees with a stream of blood coming from his forehead. The crowd gasped.

Chris righted Owen, and saw Harry's forehead. In a panic, he looked at Sophie, and immediately started his lines from halfway through. "I'll love you forever!"

He unfortunately spoke this line just as a large man in a leather biker jacket stepped in front of Sophie. The biker stopped, looked Chris up and down, scratched his beard, and swore at him. Jim took exception to this, and swore at the biker, and then attempted to explain it was a theatrical performance and the biker was interrupting...as the biker threw him on to the fruit stall. Lillian jumped on the biker's back, and wrapped her hands around his neck. The biker thought she was trying to choke him. Lillian thought she was riding a horse.

Zoe screamed. Emily suddenly appeared from behind the fishmonger's stall, shouting, "Get off that old lady! How dare you touch her!"

When the police eventually arrived, everyone was in a heap on the floor, except for Emily who was standing on the fruit stall throwing punches at anyone who came near her.

***

It wasn't all bad. For a start, Anne didn't get arrested. Everyone else did, but Anne hadn't actually been involved in a physical way, as she was still behind the fruit and veg stall. It fell to her to try and get everyone released.

"But officer, you must understand, this was a performance in aid of a local theatre group! We meant no harm!"

"I hear what you are saying, Mrs Butler, but the fact remains that no-one had authorised it, and it almost caused a riot. Any public performance on the marketplace has to be authorised by the council, and this performance was not authorised. In fact, it caused a disturbance. Especially as everyone thought those two were actual lunatics. The bloke with the eyebrows and the old woman."

"You mean Owen and Lillian, and they are not lunatics. Well, one of them might be, but they were never properly tested. Jim, my husband, deals with all the council matters, all permissions and that. If you ask him, I'm sure he'll tell you that."

"We did ask him. He slapped his hand to his forehead and said a word I'm not going to repeat. Apparently, he was too busy 'balancing the books and rehearsing' to remember to get in touch with the council. Everyone's always too busy."

"Oh no...oh Jim! How could he forget something so important!"

"It's not for me to say, Mrs Butler. The good news is that Mr Johnson, the large fella that Mrs Lovelace and Miss Ravenscroft assaulted, is not going to press charges. In fact, he thought the whole thing was hilarious, apart from the bit where Mr Crumple told him he loved him, but he eventually saw the funny side of that too."

"So what happens now?"

"Well, just a little bit of paperwork to do, and then they're all free to go..."

The doors of the police station burst open, and Tom McLean, facing glowing red, charged through them.

"What the hell is going on, Anne? My daughter has been arrested, and you, and no doubt your fat husband, are to blame!"

"And who might you be, sir?" asked the desk sergeant.

"I am Tom McLean, father of Zoe McLean, local entrepreneur and businessman, member of the Chamber of Commerce and regular donater to charity."

"And no doubt head of the Magic Circle too, sir. Miss McLean is to be released in a few moments time, I just need to..."

"All you need to do, *sunshine*, is let her out and let me take her home. I've got your badge number, and I know where Mrs Butler lives."

"Was that a threat, sir? Directed at an innocent bystander?"

"She's not innocent!"

"And that's not a denial, sir."

"Whatever! Let my daughter out. I'll be outside waiting in the car!"

Tom turned to storm out the door.

"Outside sir? Is that on the double yellow lines, sir? You might want to move that before one of my colleagues spots you, sir."

"I've still got your badge number, officer," said Tom has he walked out.

"And I've got my eye on *you*, **sir**."

***

The Players, sans Zoe, regrouped that evening in the upstairs room at the Tavern.

"I am so sorry," said Lillian. "I don't know what came over me."

"I do," said Owen. "My bottle of gin, that's what. I hope you're going to replace it."

"I hope neither of you go near the gin for a while!" said Harry. He touched the bandage on his head. "You pair drinking gives me a headache!"

Sophie and Chris sat next to each other, still stunned by the events of the day.

"I just can't understand how it went so bad so quickly. One minute we were acting, the next minute we were fighting," said Sophie. "I just don't get it."

"Well, the one thing I can take away from it," said Chris, "is that my delivery of lines has a certain effect on people. Specifically, they seem to take offence to it. And to me."

"I still think you're lovely," said Sophie.

Harry cleared his throat. "Anyone want a drink before I throw up? If someone else is buying, I'll have a coke, because I can't have anything stronger due to the painkillers. And I think someone else *should* buy, as I was the only one who was properly physically injured."

"My knuckles got scraped really bad," said Emily.

"That's because you were punching everybody else."

***

Emily was one of the first to leave. She'd had a tiring day, as anyone who has tried boxing could tell you. Sophie was ready to go with her, but Emily told her to stay, as she was clearly enjoying the company of Chris. Sophie agreed, and pointed out that Emily "Rocky" Ravenscroft was obviously capable of looking after herself should any trouble arise.

Emily considered walking over to take a look at the hall. After all the stories she'd heard, she was quite keen to take a look for herself. Although she'd been in the hall many times before, it seemed that the place had become very active recently. Emily had an aunt who swore she was psychic, and this aunt had claimed many times that the hall was haunted. Emily thought the aunt was a bit mad, which was probably true. Emily didn't want to know if psychic ability was a family trait, but there again, she kind of *did* want to know.

She dismissed the thought. If she didn't know if she wanted to know if she was psychic, how could she be psychic? She just didn't know.

She looked over her shoulder, towards the hall. It sat in darkness, the only illumination coming from a nearby street lamp. And then she saw a flash of light from *inside*. At first, it looked like the beam from a torch, but it got larger and larger, until it almost filled one of the upstairs windows. Slowly, it faded and receded, until it was distinctly in the shape of a man. A tall, glowing man.

He waved.

She waved back.

In her head she heard a faint voice. It spoke to her.

"Hello, you. Think you're on my wavelength. I

need you to look in the toilet."

Emily screamed, and ran all the way home.

ADAM G NEWTON

Chapter 10

The first step in the sales process is to get your foot in the door. Once you've found a way to get that far, closing the sale is just a matter of persistence. The hard part is the introduction - it's not easy to approach someone cold and sell to them.

Lillian was fully aware of this. She also knew she had a great way to get her foot in the door. It was a sunny but cool Monday afternoon, and life around Blackworth market was ticking along as normal, with the events of Saturday just a memory. Nobody would be expecting a second assault on the marketplace by the Bentley Hill Players, but that was exactly what Lillian intended. This time she hoped it would happen without the involvement of the local constabulary.

A bell tinkled as she opened the door in to the first shop located on the marketplace. The plan of attack was simple; start at one end, and work all the way round to the other. This first shop sold fabric, and curtains, and other things you could make from fabric. Like more curtains.

"Hellooooo!", she called.

The shop's interior was quite dark. Displays of different styles of fabric filled the windows, so the main source of light inside was from a flickering fluorescent tube overhead. A small mousey woman appeared from behind a beaded curtain. She wore thick glasses, a cream sweater, and a brown skirt. If she hadn't worked here, she would certainly have worked in a library. As a historian. Upstairs. In a dark corner.

"Hello, madam. How may I help you?"

"I was just passing by, and I suddenly came over all strange. You wouldn't have a chair I could use, would you?"

"But of course! Come with me," said the woman, taking Lillian's arm. "Sit as long as you like."

She took Lillian through the bead curtain, and sat her at a table in a small kitchenette.

"Thank you. That's much better. I...I don't suppose I could trouble you for a cup of tea?"

"Of course, my dear! I'll boil the kettle right now!"

Lillian smiled as the woman filled the kettle with fresh water. Not only did she have her foot in the door, she had her bum in a seat, a tasty cuppa on the way, and with a bit of luck, she would also receive the sympathy vote. And if she played her cards right, there might be a biscuit, too.

"Did you hear about the disturbance on the market on Saturday?" asked Lillian.

"I did! There were so many arrests! So awful!"

"I know, I was there."

"Oh, you poor thing!"

"No, it's worse than that. I was one of the ones who were arrested!"

"Really? How's that then?"

"Well, you see, I'm a member of the Bentley Hill Players. We are a small amateur theatrical group, and we were giving a performance on the market to let people know about our new play. And then, all of a sudden, this big hairy brute comes out of nowhere and professes his love for one of our leading men. Well, next thing you know, he chasing after him, trying to give him a kiss, and I step in front of him, and smack him with my handbag. The coppers turn up, and arrest everyone in sight. I don't know what happened to that hairy fella, but the Players were all released without charge."

"That's awful!" said the woman, pouring the tea in to two waiting cups.

"I know! I'm nearly a hundred, and got no special consideration! And all I wanted to do was to help my friends promote our show. Tickets sales have been very slow."

"Oh, that is a shame."

"It is. A great shame. I might not make it long enough to perform again..."

"Oh no!"

"...because I am very old, you know. Weak, too. So, so weak. It's cold in here, isn't it?"

"I didn't think so..."

"...oh....lights fading....getting dark....so cold..."

"Are you all right missus?!"

"....low sugar...might need a biscuit..."

"I've got some ginger snaps. Hold on."

"...any bourbons?"

"Yes. Here you go."

"Why thank you. That's much better," said

Lillian, before even taking a single bite.

"Oh good. You poor woman. I'm sorry, I forgot to ask your name?"

"Lillian Lovelace. You may have heard of me."

"No, can't say that I have."

"It's not my fault that *you* are uncultured."

"Beg pardon?"

"I said the tea is *lovely*."

"Oh, good! My name is Ruth. My husband and I own this shop, such as it is."

"I'll tell you what it is, it's dark. But you, Ruth, are an angel, sent to help an old woman like me. I have a favour to ask, if it's not too much trouble. I mean, you have been so kind already."

"Ask away, Mrs Lovelace."

"Well, as my troubles this weekend started trying to get word out about our show, could you possibly help? I have this," she said, pulling a flyer out of her handbag. "I wonder if you could display it in your window? Think of it as...a dying old lady's final wish."

"Of course, Mrs Lovelace! I would be proud to do so!"

"Brilliant!"

Lillian shovelled the rest of the bourbons in to her mouth, and washed them down with a big swig of tea. She jumped to her feet.

"Right, been lovely chatting, but I must get on. Thank you for your hospitality!"

She quickly walked out through the curtain, and straight out the front door of the shop, leaving Ruth completely bewildered with a flyer in her hand. Ruth shrugged, sighed, and started looking for some tape to put the flyer in the window.

Outside, Lillian marched to the door of the next shop, which just happened to be a cafe.

"Hmm. Might get a better cup of tea in here. And a better class of biscuit."

She stooped a little, and shuffled inside.

"Hellooo! I was just passing by, and suddenly came over all strange. Can anyone help a dying old lady?"

***

If ghosts come out at night, thought Dave Sweet,

then the best time to avoid them is during the day.
Amongst the many tasks Dave performed at the
community hall, general cleaning was the most
time consuming. Sweeping from top to bottom,
cleaning the bathrooms, dusting, and so on. By
now, Dave was intimately familiar with the
timetable of use for the hall, and had figured out a
way to avoid being there late at night. Once
everyone had gone, he'd lock up, and return the
following day before that hall was next due to be
used, and tidy up then.

And so it happened that on this particular
Monday afternoon, Dave was working as hard as
he could. He'd miscalculated exactly what time he
needed to start, and now only had 5 minutes before
the Ladies of East & South Blackworth Open
Society arrived to knit something and chat about
Eastenders.

Dave had saved his least favourite job until
last. Although they usually weren't *that* bad, Dave
absolutely hated cleaning out the toilets in the hall.
And to make matters worse, the ghostly voice he'd
heard seemed to have some kind of attachment to
the toilets.

He had just finished mopping the floor when
he heard a loud bang. Dave froze. This was how it

started. And then, he heard a voice - no, wait, several voices. It was the Ladies! No need to panic.

Dave shuffled his mop and bucket out the door, and met some of the Ladies in the corridor outside.

"Hello there! Everything's spick and span!"

"Glad to hear it!" one of the Ladies answered.

"*BUT!*" said another voice. "*THERE IS A PROBLEM!*"

Dave looked around, startled, trying to find the source of the voice.

"What's the problem?" asked the same Lady.

"*I NEED ONE OF YOU TO GO IN THE TOILET WITH ME.*"

"What?"

"*I'VE BEEN HERE SO LONG, AND NO-ONE WILL GO IN THE TOILET WITH ME. COME IN, AND I'LL SHOW YOU WHAT TO DO!*"

"If you value your job, you'll apologise for that!"

"It's not me!" said Dave.

"Then who is it, wise guy?"

"*ME!*"

A bluish mist slowly materialised in front of the door to the gents. The top part gradually developed a nose, then some eyes, and then a mouth, all partially transparent, all blue.

"*HELLO!*" said the face, with a smile.

Dave and the Ladies screamed in unison, and every last one ran out of the building.

ADAM G NEWTON

Chapter 11

"Look at that, Harry!", said Chris.

"What?"

"In the window. The flyer."

Chris and Harry were sitting facing each other, devouring a pizza between them, in one of the cafes on Blackworth marketplace. A Monday evening treat. But it didn't have to be Monday for Chris and Harry to be enjoying pizza.

"S*reyalp llih yeltneb*, or something? Is it Arabic? Wait...it's backwards? Oh! It's us!"

"I know, right? How did that get there?"

"I guess Jim must have been round, grovelling. Must have taken a lot of work after Saturday. I've never had such fun!"

"Really? I accidentally profess my love for a biker, and nearly get beat up, and you get a chunk knocked out of your head. What do you normally do to pass the time?"

"Hang out with you. Like I said, it was fun!"

"Well that's very kind of you. But seriously, I don't think this show is going to work. Look at it this way - we've not sold anywhere near enough tickets, we've got a bad reputation in Blackworth after the brawl, and I still can't say any of the names in the thing."

"True enough, but your love life is on the up."

"I don't know about that. I don't know about anything. Agh! The only thing I'm sure of is that this pepperoni pizza is tasty."

"This *pepperoni pizza* is ham, Chuckles. Ham and pineapple. Do you even *do* fruit? What's the problem, anyway? I mean, with Sophie, not the pizza."

"I don't know. I like her, I really do, but...it just sort of happened, you know? I didn't plan it, so I'm not sure what to do."

"If I were your age again, oh *such fun*. There will come a day, young man, when the women will not be throwing themselves at you. You will be a wrinkled shell of your former self, living alone, feeding the cat from next door in the hope of making a new friend. You will be a sad, strange, little man, most likely with a drinking problem."

"So you're saying if I don't get married in the next 24 hours I'll turn in to Owen?"

He nodded. "That is indeed the short version."

"Shut up and eat your pizza."

***

Harry and Chris decided to call it a night at around 10PM, and walked all the way down the hill together. Their conversation moved from one thing to another, but centred mainly around Sophie and the lack of ticket sales.

They arrived at Harry's house.

"So, I'll see you tomorrow then?"

"I guess so, yeah. Got nothing else to do!" said Chris, laughing.

"What about taking Sophie out somewhere?"

"Mmm. Yeah, so, nothing else to do."

"What is *wrong* with you?"

"I think I'm giving up, pretty much. I don't think I'm ready to commit to Sophie, and if we aren't going to be able to put this show on, there'll be no reason to see her. And no rehearsals either, so

I'll be free to do as I please."

"I think you're making a mistake there. She's a lovely girl. And we'll do the show, somehow."

"Well, let's agree to disagree then.

"No, let's not."

"No, I meant about the Sophie thing and the show, not disagree with me agreeing with you to disagree."

"Mate, I think you're wonderful, but you really need to get your head straight. Love and kisses to your mother. See you tomorrow!"

"Yeah, love and kisses to your gran, you tart. Laters, taters."

Harry went in through his front door, and gave Chris a wave as he went on his way. Chris waited until the door was firmly closed, and started walking in the opposite direction, towards Sophie's house.

***

"Who is that at this time of night?" thundered Sophie's dad. "They'd better not be selling anything."

He opened the door, and there stood Chris.

"Good evening, Mr Patterson. The only thing I am selling is religion. Can I interest you in a small portion of godliness?"

"No, you can't. If you're here to see Sophie, you've got five minutes, in the kitchen. And then you can get home, capische?"

"Understood."

"*SOPHIE!*"

Seconds later, Sophie came down the stairs and met Chris in the kitchen. She threw her arms around his neck, and hugged him tightly.

"Hiya! What are you doing here so late? I was going to text you before bed."

"I've got a lot of stuff on my mind right now, so I wanted to come and see you."

"Oh?"

"Yeah, it's mostly like, er, you. And the show."

"Me?"

"Yeah."

"What's wrong with me?"

"Nothing. Something. I don't know!"

"…Are you breaking up with me?"

There was a long silence. Chris looked deeply in to Sophie's eyes.

"Er.......no?"

"Oh wow, I actually thought you were!"

She kissed him on the lips, and Chris relaxed. It was all going to be fine.

***

Chris was there for more than the promised five minutes, but Sophie's parents were too busy watching the TV to notice. However, when the show finished, Mr Patterson took no time at all to send Chris on his way.

"You're a lovely lad, I'm sure," he said. "But only during daylight hours. G'night!"

Chris walked all the way home with a smile on his face, and was about to walk in through his own front door when a thought occurred to him. *What if this whole ghost thing is a plot by Tom McLean to scare the townsfolk away from the hall*?

That would make it easy to sell, as there would be no-one to object to the sale. No-one would want to go near it. Except for Christopher Crumple, right now. He walked straight down to the hall.

The very moment he reached the end of the path to the door, all his confidence left him. He pulled his phone from his pocket, and turned the screen on to illuminate the ground at his feet.

If this is a fake haunting, then there'll be trip wires or floor sensors or something, designed to set the special effects off.

He walked slowly up the path, staring intently at the patch of ground illuminated by his phone. *A few pebbles, a bit of cracked concrete. A few leaves, a twig. A splash of paint, a foot. Another crack, and...wait...a foot?*

He tilted the screen of the phone.

Yep. A foot. How peculiar. Attached to a leg, and a waist. And a chest. And a neck. Oh, I really hope there's a head on this. Oh there is. And it's smiling. Where do I know that face from? And why is he blue?

"WELL HELLO!"

"Um, hi?"

"ARE YOU OF SOUND MIND?"

"I thought so until a couple of minutes ago..."

"*GOOD, GOOD! THERE WAS A MAN WHO LOOKED LIKE AN UPENDED BROOM HERE EARLIER ALONG WITH SOME LADIES. THEY WERE NOT OF SOUND MIND. HOWEVER, I DID MIND THE SOUND THEY MADE! DO YOU GET IT? THE SOUND! HAHA!*"

"Not really, no..."

"*NEVER MIND, MAYBE HUMOUR IS NOT YOUR STRONG POINT. ARE YOU A COURAGEOUS YOUNG MAN?*"

"I like to think I am."

"*EXCELLENT! I HAVE A QUEST FOR YOU TO UNDERTAKE! WILL YOU DO MY BIDDING?*"

"Maybe. Depends. What is it that you want?"

"*I WANT YOU TO FIND SOMETHING PRECIOUS TO ME. SOMETHING I HAD A LONG TIME AGO. BUT I LOST IT. I WANT YOU TO HOLD IT. YOU'LL KNOW WHAT TO DO WITH IT!*"

"And what is it?"

"*IT IS PRECIOUS, AND IT IS HEAVY. COME WITH ME...TO THE TOILET! JUST STICK YOUR HEAD IN! PLEASE! HEY! HEY! COME BACK! OH,*"

BUM."

Chris didn't stop running until he got to Harry's house. He pounded on the door until Harry answered.

"Wassup? I was in bed?"

"Went see Sophie. Kiss. Home. No, hall. Looked for tricks, found feet. Trick or feet. Ghost wants me to put my head in the toilet to look at his precious. HELP!"

"Did you want to come in for a bit?"

"I think that might help."

Chapter 12

"The thing is, Zoe, sweetie, the more people that use that place, the more chance of them protesting the sale, the more chance the council will stick their noses in. And I can do without that. So I want you to leave the Players."

"But dad, I really enjoy it! I could still be an actress, you know!"

"Of course you could. But thinking about it, you actually have a privileged position, don't you? You could be my man on the inside!"

"*Man*, dad?"

"Woman then. Sow seeds of discontent. Break the group up! It'll give you a chance to practice your acting."

"Do you mean *lying* rather than acting, dad?"

"I would never advocate lying. But yes."

"No, dad."

"I'll make it worth your while."

"How? I'm not easily bought dad, I'm not like that."

"With the money we'd make from selling the hall, I could buy you a field."

"A field? What would I do with that? Host a cricket match for you and your mates?"

"No, but you'd need somewhere to keep your horse, wouldn't you?"

"Horse? Are you OK, dad? I don't have a horse!"

"Not yet, you don't. But the hall isn't sold yet, either."

"Oh, I *see*. Tell me more."

"Well, from what I've heard, there are four main characters in this show. And I must say they all have ridiculous names."

"I know that, dad."

"Well, the main four are played by you, Sophie, Owen and Christopher. I'll make sure Owen gets a bottle of whiskey outside his door every morning, and that should take care of him. He won't be able to remember his lines. He might not even turn up. Which leaves Sophie and Christopher."

"Who, the two love birds?"

"That is what I've been told. So the best thing to do, in my opinion, is to get them at each others throats. A bit of he said, she said. What do you think?"

"I think it's a bit unethical to mess with people like that."

"One horse would be lonely on it's own, don't you think? Normally better in pairs."

"I could do something, I guess. But I think you need to help. Here's what I have in mind..."

***

Chris got home from work at the usual time, and was surprised to find Tom McLean's car parked outside his house. He ambled over, and knocked on the window. The window rolled down, and Tom was revealed, grinning like a Cheshire cat.

"Hello Chris! Just here on a social visit!"

"Uh, righto, Mr McLean. Is there something I can help you with?"

"No, no, like I said, social. Just wondered how you are getting on with learning your lines and all that?"

"Fine, thanks. Actually, I'm glad you're here. I need to talk to you about the hall..."

"...yes, me too. I'm selling it, and no-one will stop me. That's really the reason I'm here, just to let you know that."

"It's haunted."

"Of course it is. This is your play, right? *The Ghost in the Cupboard*?"

"It's *Under the Stairs*, actually, but no. It's actually really properly haunted."

"No, it isn't. Is it?"

"Yep. A blue man who wants to take people in the toilet and do unspeakable things to their heads."

Tom's smile remained on his face, but it was only his mouth that was smiling. His eyes showed concern. Tom was not in any way afraid of ghosts. He was however afraid of people who thought they could see ghosts.

"A blue man, in the toilets?"

"Yep."

"And you've seen him in the toilets?"

"No, he was outside, trying to get me to go with him."

"So a blue man tried to pick you up on the street, and tried to take you in the toilets?"

"Just my head."

"Do you realize how stupid that sounds?"

"Not really, no."

"It doesn't matter. The important thing is, you know that I'm selling the hall."

"Why do you keep telling me that?"

"So you *know*. I just wanted to point out that when that place is gone, you'll have nothing to do at least half the nights of the week, will you?"

"Well, no."

"I could offer you a night security job at my factory."

"I already have a job..."

"But I'd pay double what you're getting now. But I can only afford that once the hall is gone. Interested?"

"Well, kind of. I mean the money would be great to have...."

"And I'm sure *Sophie* would think it was a good idea. Even though you wouldn't see her much."

"Why not?"

"Because you'd be working nights. But you'd have all day to do whatever you wanted. Just think about it. I'll be seeing you around, I'm sure. Ta-ta."

Tom started the engine, flashed Chris a wink, rolled the window up, and drove off.

"He's a weirdo. He's clearly a weirdo. A weirdo who is intent on selling a building, and needed to let me know. Weirdo."

***

Tom's next stop was Sophie's house. He parked at the end of the drive, and knocked on the door. Sophie answered after a few seconds.

"Oh, hi. Are you here to see my dad?"

"Nope, just wanted to tell you a couple of things. I'm selling the hall, and I've offered Chris a well-paying job based on the sale going through. He's agreed to it, and so he's going to work for me. I'll own *him*, but I won't own the hall any more. Thought it was best that you heard it from me.

Tootles!"

Tom gave a silly little wave and pranced off up the drive to his car. Sophie wrinkled her nose, scratched her head, and closed the door.

"That can't be right. Chris loves the group, he'd never do that."

She pulled out her phone, and went to the texting app.

Hey, Tom's just been here. Says he offered you a job.

A few seconds elapsed, and the phone went *bong*.

Yes. Says he's selling the hall.

So you encouraged him?

No. Don't know why he told me that.

He said the job was based on the sale.

It is. And I won't be able to see you.

What? Why?

Because of the time.

But it's only early.

No, for when I'd be working.

So you accepted! I can't deal with you right now!

And with that, Sophie turned her phone off.

***

Chris went straight round to Harry's house, hoping together they could make sense of the text conversation.

"So I don't know what's up with her, Harry."

"Don't you think talking to her would have been better? She might have misunderstood what you meant..."

"Well of course she did. She's a woman, everything I say is designed to be misunderstood. Can you see why I just want to give up sometimes?"

"Not really, no!" said Harry, laughing.

"Aw man, it's not funny. I think I'm just gonna have a quiet one tonight. I'll leave her to cool down a bit. An argument is the last thing I need. I'm going home again, having my tea, and a shower, and I'm going to watch rubbish on the telly all night."

"Have fun mate. I might ring you in a bit to see if you've had any revelations."

"I doubt I will have, but OK. Sees-ya!"

ADAM G NEWTON

Chapter 13

Chris was bored. Tremendously, ridiculously, totally bored. He'd eaten his tea, taken a shower, put on his pyjamas, and settled down to watch whatever the TV could throw at him. Unfortunately, it turned out to be a combination of all the worst TV shows ever made.

By 8 o'clock, he'd had enough. He dragged himself from his armchair, and pressed the 'OFF' button on the TV. As the screen went black there was a knock at the door.

"Yes! Harry to the rescue! I knew he'd pop round!"

As Chris charged to the door, a thought crossed his mind. *What if it's not Harry? Here I am, in my Pjs, about to open the door to a potential stranger. Well, too late to change now.*

He removed the security chain and swung the door open.

"Harry! I...oh. Hi, Zoe."

"Hi Chris! You look...ready for bed," she said, trying not to look directly at the picture of Spongebob Squarepants on the pyjamas.

"Yeah...uh...I was gonna have an early night. You want to come in for a minute?"

"Yes, that would be nice."

Without forgetting his manners, Chris offered Zoe a cup of coffee, which she gladly accepted. He made one for each of them, and they sat in the living room to drink them.

"Look, first of all, I want to apologise for my dad. Sometimes, he gets a bit carried away, and sometimes he shouts, but that's not really him. Inside, he's like the nicest person in the world, but there's some sort of filter in him that only lets the angry stuff out."

"You don't have to apologise on behalf of your dad. In fact, he offered me a job today. I admit, he did it in a kind of passive-agressive way, but I see what you mean. It's like the thought was there, but it came out as anger!"

Zoe nodded as she had experienced this kind of thing first hand. "But I wanted to say something else too. It's a bit tricky, though."

"I've had a bit of a tricky day, so I think I'll

cope. Spill it."

"Watching you rehearsing with Sophie, I've seen a different side of you. You're kind, considerate. You're not as abrasive as I thought you were."

"Thanks, I think. Sophie might not feel the same right now, though. Am I really abrasive?"

"See, I knew I'd make a mess of it. What I'm trying to say is, I think I'm falling for you."

"Right."

"Did you hear what I said?"

"Yes. Wait, you mean, falling, as in, like, you like me?"

"That *is* what it means."

Zoe slid across the sofa so she was right next to the armchair Chris sat in. She reached over and put her hand on top of his, adopting her best puppy-dog-eyes expression.

She continued, "I know you've felt the same way for some time. You're always struggling with your words around me, being more clumsy than normal. I've seen you looking at me."

"I hap a lot of um ah. What? Words? Hum? Can I get you a biscuit?" Chris said, standing up and trying to get to the kitchen. He tripped over the coffee table in his haste, and knocked over both cups that were on it. "Ah! Must get towel. Be right back!"

He extracted his hand from Zoe's, leapt over the table, and ran to the kitchen. He looked around for something to mop up the spilled coffee, and finally settled on a shirt from the washing pile. He turned back towards the living room, and walked straight in to Zoe.

"Oh, sorry! I didn't hear you foll..."

Her arms were suddenly wrapped around him and her lips were on his. For a brief moment, he enjoyed the sensation. And then an image of Sophie flashed in his mind, and the reality of the situation hit him. He pushed her away.

"What ya doing? You can't come in my house, spill my coffee, and kiss me like, like, like, a kissing thing! You hardly gave me the time of day last week!"

"Things change! Hey! Hold on, I didn't spill the coffee!"

"You may as well have done. Shift!"

He pushed his way past her and made his way back to the living room, where he dropped to his knees and started to mop up the coffee.

Zoe followed him, and sat behind him on the sofa. She lazily lifted her finger, and ran it up and down the back of his neck.

"Gerroff! That tickles!"

He turned to admonish her further, and again she was on him. Realizing he could do nothing to dissuade her, he rose to his feet, lifting Zoe with him. He carried her in a reverse-piggyback position to the front door, opened it, and dropped her on the step outside.

"Hey! What's wrong?"

"Everything about this. You can tell your dad a big fat *no* from me, and you can have a bit of the same yourself. I am *not* a piece of meat."

Zoe grunted loudly and stamped her foot.

"You'll be sorry, Crumple, mark my words. Gah!"

She stormed off down the path, and slammed the gate behind her. Chris stood for a moment, looking after her.

"It never rains but it flamin' well pours," he said.

An elderly man walking up the street glanced

his way, and stopped to take it all in. Chris stood on the doorstep, still in his pyjamas. He wore no shoes, had coffee stains on both knees, his Spongebob top had ridden up to expose his midriff, his hair was all over the place, and his face was covered in lipstick.

"Evening son. Is it Halloween already?"

Chapter 14

The weeks flew by, and the rehearsal went as well as could be expected. Chris was annoyed with Zoe, whilst his relationship with Sophie was, at best, rocky. They spoke and were civil, but could hardly be considered an item. The show was constantly under a dark cloud due to the impending sale of the hall, which deeply affected the mood of all the Players.

The first rehearsal in the hall was just a couple of days away, and would be followed by a dress rehearsal in just a week. In theory everything would by then be ready for opening night. Despite Lillian's best efforts, ticket sales had remained slow, but at least the flyers in the windows had got some people talking about the show.

Sophie lay on her bed, reading a book - a romantic novel – which left her wondering why life never worked the way it did in stories. The handsome prince was always there to save the day and give the princess the life she deserved. *Why isn't Chris like that? Why is he a bit useless?*

Her phone buzzed on her bedside table. She sighed in realization that the real world required her attention, and she would have to leave the bulging muscles and rooms covered in rose petals behind.

It was a text from Chris.

I CAN'T GO ON

Her stomach dropped. *Oh no! He's having suicidal thoughts!*

The phone buzzed again.

STAGE WHEN THERE'S A GHOST

She rolled her eyes and pressed the button to call Chris. It rang out and went to the answering service. She hung up without leaving a message. *Obviously doesn't want to talk about it.*

Sophie returned to reading her book, and within seconds the phone started to ring. She sighed and put the book down. It was Chris on the phone.

"Hello?"

"Uh, hi. Sorry I didn't answer. I, er, didn't know what to say."

"Well *hello* is often a good start."

"Sorry. Hello. Look, I can't do this any more!"

"Me neither! These last few weeks have been the worst of my life!"

"So you feel the same! Sophie, I am so pleased that it's not just me."

"I am so relieved. You can't believe how upset I've been."

"I've not been upset. More scared really."

"Scared? You little silly. You could just have talked to me and we could have worked it out."

"I guess. But how can we deal with it?"

"Just forget about it."

"It's a bit hard when it stands there and looks at you."

"I...what?"

"The ghost. He stands there and looks at you. And tells you he's going to put your head in the toilet."

There was silence on the line.

"*Hello*? Sophie?"

"You actually rang me to tell me you can't go

on stage because of a *ghost*? I thought we were getting back together!"

"Er...can we just deal with one thing at once right now?"

"I was doing."

"Yeah, but it was the wrong thing."

"Chris, I still have feelings for you. An argument isn't going to change that. But you've got your priorities backwards."

"Well, tell me what to do about the ghost then!"

"I've *never* seen a ghost in that hall, and I've been there as many times as you have. Probably more. I think there's a problem in your head."

"Are we still talking about the ghost now?"

"I don't know any more. If you back out of the show now, you're going to let a lot of people down, just because of something you probably imagined. At the moment, you've only let me down."

"Sorry."

"Stop saying sorry!"

"Sorry."

"Just get yourself to the rehearsal on Tuesday.

We'll talk then. There's nothing to worry about."

"OK. Thanks. I will. See ya!"

Chris hung up.

"....love you..."

Chapter 15

Chris stood at the end of the path leading to the front door of the community hall. He looked at the ground, and then at the trees and bushes. He looked to the upstairs windows, and then at the doors. He looked at the ground again.

"What are you doing?"

He looked over his shoulder to see Sophie standing there, arms crossed in front of her.

"Checking."

"Checking what?"

"That the ghost is clear."

"The what?"

"The coast. I meant the coast."

"There isn't a ghost here – look! Nothing at all. Now, come on in."

She pushed past him, grabbed his jacket sleeve on the way, and pulled him up the path behind her.

They entered the hall to a scene of complete chaos. Had Dante imagined his 9 Rings of Hell as an amateur theatre production, this would have been it. Harry was on the stage, attempting to prop up an 8 foot tall scenery board by himself. An old record player was at the front of the stage, playing very loud jazz music. Owen and Lillian were on the main floor of the hall, dancing around in circles to the music. Jim sat on a chair to the left of the stage, script in one hand, scratching his head with the other. Zoe leaned against a wall, dressed in denim jeans with a matching jacket, engrossed in something on her phone. Anne was pacing back and forth across the stage, and Emily was following her, wearing a peach dress that made her look as if she were a bridesmaid at a royal wedding. Dave Sweet stood in the centre of the hall, leaning on his brush, surveying the scene.

"You know, sometimes I've wondered, *what would living in an asylum be like*? Well now I know." said Chris.

Owen and Lillian were spinning faster and faster, getting more and more out of control. Finally, Owen spun too fast, and crashed in to the front of the stage knocking the record player flying. It landed with a loud bang on the stage, that caused

Jim to jump up in fright. He tripped and staggered across the stage, clipping Harry in the back of the knee, causing his leg to buckle, which in turn caused the scenery board to fall on him. Emily jumped out the way when the board started to fall, and slipped down the steps at the side of the stage, while Anne jumped in the opposite direction and fell over the record player. Meanwhile, Lillian was still spinning around on her own, eventually crashing in to Dave, who fell to the floor with his brush skidding across the floor. The head of the brush hit the wall next to Zoe, causing the handle to flip up and knock the phone out of her hand. Chris ran and dived to catch the phone, missed, and hit his chin on the floor instead. The phone bounced off his head and landed on the floor next to him.

Sophie looked around in amazement.

"I think you were right, Chris," she said. "Welcome to hell."

***

The scenery board was broken, snapped in half. Emily's dress was torn. Owen didn't realise anything untoward had happened. Things were not going well.

Chris was still struggling with pronouncing all of the names, and Harry had yet another head injury. Jim was in panic mode.

"There's no way we are going to be ready in time. Opening night is Friday, we don't stand a chance. This is the show that's never going to get shown."

"C'mon Jim," said Harry. "You can't give up now. I'm sure there have been more than a few setbacks in the history of this group. This is just a small bump in the road. The scenery can be fixed, everyone is OK, and the biggest problem is getting Chris to get his words out right."

"I am *trying*!"

"Right then," said Jim. "Let's try the first scene in act two and see how we get on. At least if it's not a complete disaster I'll feel like I have something to work with."

The stage cleared except for Owen, who stepped to the front and hunched his left shoulder up.

"Tonight is the night in which my lady-love shall win. Her inheritance will be all that it is meant to be, and I shall be her rock to lean on. But first a little murder, a little intrigue, and a lot of lying. To the home of dear Priscilla!"

Owen took large strides across the stage, and squatted on the right hand side.

"It is a noble thing that I do, to give the woman that I love all that she desires!"

He rose, and walked to the opposite side, where he raised his arms above his head.

"But lo – who approaches?"

Jim walked awkwardly on to the stage.

"It's at this point I'm meant to come up through the trap door, but it's jammed at the moment. Dave said he can fix it in time for the dress rehearsal, so fingers crossed. Anyway, I come up through the trap door and do my lines. Ahem. It is I, your worst nightmare, the thing under your bed, the thing that goes bump in the night!"

There was a loud metallic creak from overhead, and everyone looked up just in time to see one of the stage lights come loose and crash down less than a foot away from Jim.

"You're not the only thing that goes bump there, Jimbo!" said Owen.

"Stone the crows! I could have died!"

"That's dedication, that is, Jimmy. Becoming an actual ghost in order to play one."

"It's not funny, Owen," said Anne. "He could have been seriously hurt."

"But....he wasn't! Bet you need a stiff drink now, don't you Jim? I'll get one for you," said Owen, wandering off out of the main hall.

"I think maybe we should take a short break," said Jim.

***

After stiff drinks were found and distributed – possibly from Owen's bag, no-one knew where they came from, but they were all in plastic cups - and everyone had calmed down, the rest of the rehearsal went surprisingly well. The only awkward part was when Chris's character professed his love for Sophie's character, which caused her to break down in tears. Zoe took a photo with her phone, which did nothing to endear her to any of the other cast members.

It was all over by 10 o'clock, and Dave was left

behind to lock up. *I can't imagine how much paperwork would have been involved if that light had hit Jim. He must have a guardian angel or something. Or it was just sheer dumb luck.*

There was a loud bang.

"What the...? I hope that's not another light."

Dave ran back in to the main hall, just in time to see a blue glowing man rise up through the stage.

"HELLO, DAVID!"

Dave stood wide-eyed and open-mouthed, unable to respond.

"GOOD TO SEE YOU AGAIN. BUT I'VE STILL NOT GOT YOU IN THE TOILETS, HAVE I?"

Dave shook his head.

"WOULD YOU LIKE TO GO IN THERE WITH ME NOW?"

Dave shook his head again, vigorously.

"SOMEBODY NEEDS TO COME IN THE TOILET WITH ME. IF NOT YOU, WHOM?"

Dave shrugged his shoulders.

"I NEED TO GET IT OUT, AND I CAN'T TOUCH IT WITH MY GHOSTLY HANDS. IT WILL

SOLVE ALL YOUR PROBLEMS!"

Dave nodded, now with an uncertain look on his face.

"GET OUT OF MY SIGHT. I NEED TO FIND SOMEONE WHO ACTUALLY CARES!"

Dave nodded, and ran. He paused only to lock the front door behind him, and ran off up the street. He passed Owen moment later.

"Owen! The spirits are out tonight! Run!"

"Will do, Davey boy! I always run when there's spirits on offer. Are we talking whiskey? Vodka? Something else? Your place or mine?"

Chapter 16

Just 24 hours remained until the curtain went up on opening night, and most of the cast were already praying that the dress rehearsal went well. And as if by magic, everything seemed to click.

Chris got every name out perfectly. Sophie didn't break down in tears. Zoe seemed to be almost pleasant to people. Owen seemed sober, which was a trick he had learned whilst working as a driving instructor, but hadn't used in quite some time.

Nobody talked about the ghost. Nobody dared. It wasn't that the ghost was so horrific that the mere mention of it would scare everyone in to silence, but more that no-one wanted to admit to even being a tiny bit afraid of it. And some just didn't want to mention it for fear of being called insane – after all, surely the ghost isn't real...is it?

The scene before the big entrance of Jim as the ghost was rehearsed and performed to perfection. Not a person out of place, not a word wrong. Jim called for everyone to take a short break whilst he went under the stage with Dave to get a crash course on operating the trapdoor mechanism.

"Now, you have to be careful," said Dave. "The platform is wooden and a bit shaky, but if you hold on tight, you'll be OK. You have grip *this*....and wind *this*....and [WHUMP] *there you go*!"

The last part of the sentence was muffled as Dave was now on the stage. Jim stepped on the platform, grabbed *that* and wound *the other*, and [WHUMP] all of a sudden he too was on the stage.

"That's quite exhilarating really! Right, places everyone, let's do this. Remember, I can't give any pointers as I'll be below deck. And speak up so I can hear my cue to appear!"

Jim went back under the stage as the rest of the cast got in position. They began almost immediately.

The first part of the scene involved almost everyone being on stage at the same time, thumping around and dancing, as the scene depicted the occurrences during and after a party. Gradually, the party-goers leave, with only Sophie remaining on stage.

She reached her last line before the appearance

of the ghost, and turned to face the trapdoor.

"...if only there were some way to know."

A pause. Nothing.

"I SAID....if only there were some way to know."

Nothing.

"JIM. IF ONLY THERE WERE SOME WAY TO KNOW!"

There was a loud bang, and suddenly the ghost was on the stage. He stood there, tall and straight, shimmering under the stage lights, confidently poised and sure footed.

"Whoa, that is impressive!" said Lillian.

"And loud," said Harry.

"My child," said the ghost. *"There is a way to know. You only have to ask the spirit world."*

"Are you of the spirit world?" asked Sophie.

"That I am. And I will show you wonders, such wonders. But now, come with me, and I will show you what you ask for!"

The ghost walked off stage, and Sophie followed. The curtain dropped, and Act I had gone particularly well.

The rest of the cast gave a round of applause.

"Bravo! Excellent!"

"That effect really worked well! I'm so glad we could get hold of one of those black-light-thingys." said Harry.

Sophie walked down the steps at the side of the stage, and said over her shoulder, "What now, Jim? Straight on to the next act?"

But Jim didn't answer.

"Jim?"

Harry rushed up the stairs past Sophie, and disappeared behind the curtains. He shouted, "He's not here!"

Owen ran up the stairs on the far side, and Dave opened the curtains. The stage was revealed, and the only people on the stage were Harry and Owen.

"Has he gone back down the trapdoor?"

"No," said Dave. "You can only come up it. It's a bit dodgy. You can't go down."

"Well where the heck is he?"

A muffled shout came from under the stage.

"I'm down here you soft buggers!"

Harry rushed backstage and down the flight of stairs beyond to the entrance to the understage area. Dave, Owen and Sophie followed closely behind.

Jim lay, flat on his back, one foot on the trapdoor platform, one on the floor.

"What have you been doing?" he asked. "I think I've done me ankle in. I fell off as soon as I got on, and put my foot back to save myself, and it just went – CRACK. I'm surprised you didn't hear me shout. It hurts like a...like a..."

"Like a what?" said Sophie.

"Nothing your ears need to hear, chicken. I think I might need an ambulance."

"But you seemed alright up on the stage!" said Sophie.

"Yes, but that's before I came back down."

"But why did you come back down when we had finished the scene?"

"Finished? We didn't even get started! I've been down here since the test flight!"

The four upright cast members looked at each other.

"Seriously, Jim," said Harry. "We saw you up

there. In all your blue make up, you looked great. It was perf...oh my lord."

"What?" said Jim.

"You're not even in make up yet, are you?"

"No, I completely forgot, what with everything else!"

"Then who the heck was that on the stage?"

"I don't care! But my leg bloody well hurts! Can you get me an ambulance now, please, if it's not too much trouble, and we'll have an inquest later. Right now, we need to get my leg fixed or there's going to be no ghost in this play. Unless we rename it *The Ghost in The Wheelchair*."

Act III

Chapter 17

The ambulance arrived in good time, and the Players made a great fuss over Jim as he was taken out of the community hall. Anne was quite distraught, and didn't calm down all that much when Jim told her to "stop mithering". Harry noted that if Jim were in any kind of life-threatening state, he wouldn't be moaning quite so much, to which Anne agreed. Both Harry and Anne went with Jim to the hospital.

The remaining Players half-heartedly went through the next scene, but with three cast members missing, it hardly seemed worthwhile.

In the end, they decided to call it a night and started to make their way home. Zoe rang her father to ask for an early lift, and he agreed to come and fetch her. Everyone knew this, as even on the phone, Tom's booming voice carried well.

Tom would have to drive from the far side of Blackworth to reach the hall, and so it happened that all the other Players left before he arrived. The only two people remaining were Zoe and Dave, who had decided he was safe to do a bit of sweeping whilst there was someone else in the building.

While waiting, Zoe had a sudden urge to go to the toilet. She entered the *Ladies*, and found a cubicle with a working lock. She closed the door behind her and slid the lock over, but before she could do anything else, she was stopped in her tracks by the sound of footsteps on the hard floor outside the cubicle. They walked across the room and stopped right in front of her.

She looked down and saw the toe-end of a pair of men's boots poking under the door, softly shimmering, slightly blue.

"I don't know who you are, or what you want, but my dad will be right outside any minute now. So leave me alone!"

"SUCH SPIRIT IN ONE SO YOUNG! FEAR NOT, LITTLE ONE, I AM NOT HERE TO HARM YOU. I NEED YOUR HELP. MY NAME IS ERIC. HOW MAY I ADDRESS YOU?"

"I...I'm Zoe."

"A BEAUTIFUL NAME. GOOD EVENING, ZOE. PLEASE STEP OUT OF THE BOX AND

FOLLOW ME."

Zoe needed the toilet more than ever now, but something about the voice was so insistent that she couldn't resist opening the door and stepping out.

Outside stood a familiar-looking man, dressed in the clothes of a bygone age. Bygone, but not long forgotten. His face made Zoe's brain twitch, for she knew him from somewhere, but could not for the life of her place him.

He shimmered and was surrounded by a faint blue haze, but otherwise looked like any other person. He bowed at the waist, and touched his hand to his head as if to raise a hat, even though he was not wearing one.

"PLEASED TO MEET YOU, ZOE. NOW, COME ALONG."

He walked, and she followed. They stopped outside the end cubicle.

"60 YEARS AGO, I MADE SOME MISTAKES. I SAVED UP FOR A RAINY DAY, AND LET MY FAMILY DOWN. WHEN THAT RAINY DAY CAME, I DIED AND COULD NOT EXTRACT MY SAVINGS. MY SAVINGS ARE RIGHT THERE."

He pointed to the porcelain bowl of what looked like the oldest toilet in the world.

"In the toilet?"

*"YES. WELL, NO. NOT **IN** THE TOILET. MORE LIKE HANGING FROM IT."*

He pointed slightly higher.

"Your savings are in the water tank? How can I get up there?"

"YOU DON'T HAVE TO. LOOK AT THE CHAIN."

"I'm looking. It looks fine."

*"IT **IS** FINE. IT IS MADE OF THE FINEST GOLD YOU WILL FIND. I THINK IN YOUR CURRENT MONEY, IT IS WORTH...WHAT IS IT YOU SAY? AH YES. A **COOL HALF-MILL**."*

Zoe blinked.

"So you're telling me there's a chain worth half a million quid hanging in the toilet? How? Why?"

"I DID SOME GOOD DEALS. I INVESTED WELL. I BOUGHT GOLD, AND HAD IT FASHIONED IN TO A CHAIN. AND WHEN THE TIME CAME, I INTENDED TO SELL IT AND GIVE MY FAMILY A NEW LIFE. I BUILT THE CHAIN LINK BY LINK, A LITTLE SAVED HERE, A LITTLE SAVE THERE. IF ANYONE KNEW I HAD IT, THEY WOULD HAVE STOLEN IT. SO I HID IT IN PLAIN

SIGHT. YEAR BY YEAR, I REPLACED THE IRON LINKS WITH MY GOLD LINKS, AND WITH THE RIGHT AMOUNT OF GRIME ADDED, NO-ONE KNEW THE DIFFERENCE."

"So why is it still here? And why is it *here*, in the community hall?"

"I DIED IN THIS BUILDING, CHOKING ON A PIECE OF CAKE AT AN AFTER-SHOW PARTY. I HAD TOLD NO-ONE ABOUT THE CHAIN, SO TO THIS DAY IT REMAINS. AND IF ANYONE EVER TRIED TO INTERFERE WITH IT, I SCARED THEM AWAY."

"But that doesn't explain why it's in the community hall!"

"THIS PLACE IS SPECIAL TO ME. I WAS AN AMATEUR THESPIAN, MUCH LIKE YOURSELF. AND THIS PLACE REMAINS SPECIAL FOR REASONS OTHER THAN THE CHAIN, BUT FOR THE MOMENT I CANNOT TELL YOU WHY, AS THERE IS ANOTHER I MUST TELL FIRST. BUT FOR NOW, I NEED YOU TO TAKE THE CHAIN DOWN AND KEEP IT SAFE. I HEAR THE BUILDING IS TO BE DEMOLISHED, AND I DO NOT WISH THE CHAIN TO FALL IN TO THE WRONG HANDS."

"Of course not, no. Not the wrong hands. I'll look after it, don't you worry."

And Zoe climbed on the toilet, and started to unhitch the chain.

***

Tom walked in to the hall, looking for Zoe.

"Zoe! I've been here ten minutes now! Where are you?"

"Sorry dad! Didn't realise!" said Zoe, appearing from the main hall. "I was just looking at a few of the props for the show."

"Well, I'm sure that was very exciting. Come on now."

The McLeans left the building while Dave remained backstage, sweeping the floor. He heard the front door slam shut with a bang.

"Oh 'eck."

Dave waited.

And waited.

But no voice came.

"Ghosty? Ghosty? Are you there, Mr Spook?"

The sound of rapid footsteps came from the entrance hall, and a shimmering blue man appeared at the door.

*"YES I'M HERE, BUT YOU ARE ABSOLUTELY **USELESS**. THAT GIRL HELPED ME OUT IN THE TOILET, BUT NOW SHE'S TAKEN MY PRIZED POSSESSION AND HIDDEN IT, AND I DON'T KNOW WHERE! SAFE FOR THE LORD KNOWS HOW MANY YEARS, AND NOW IT'S GONE, JUST LIKE THAT! **IF YOU'D COME TO THE TOILET WITH ME IN THE FIRST PLACE, NONE OF THIS WOULD HAVE HAPPENED!**"*

***

The diagnosis was not good, but at least it wasn't a break. Jim had severely injured his ankle, and wouldn't be able to walk on it for several weeks, but it could have been worse. His left leg was now encased in a plaster cast right up to his knee, and he was sat in a wheelchair.

"Well this is just dandy, isn't it? From *The Ghost Under the Stairs* to *The Ghost on Wheels*. Even if I could do it on crutches, it would look ridiculous."

"You are not seriously considering going through that trapdoor on crutches, are you?" asked Harry.

"The show must go on, my friend, the show must go on."

"That's as may be, but you're in no fit state to do it."

"Well no-one else can do it! I'm the only one!"

"If only you'd had an understudy. Someone who watched you perform, and could work the trapdoor. But there just aren't enough of us."

"What about Dave?" said Anne.

"**DAVE?**" said Harry and Jim in unison.

"Yes, Dave. He's seen our rehearsals. He knows the story, he probably knows most of the lines, and I don't think he has much of a social life so he'll be available. If he'd do it, he'd be perfect."

"Fine." said Jim. "You can ask him, but it's a bit short notice, isn't it? I mean, kick off is tomorrow night, and we still need to finish of the scenery. Getting a replacement actor up to speed right now is going to be a job and a half."

***

Dave sat up. His broom was by his side, and his head hurt. He suddenly realised he was sitting in the middle of the stage at the community hall. He looked around quickly, trying to see if the blue man was still there. He wasn't.

Dave whispered, "Hello?"

No answer.

Dave scrambled to his feet, ran and jumped of the front of the stage, and hit the ground running. He tossed his broom in the store cupboard near the entrance, raced out the front door, and slammed and locked it behind him.

Not for the first time, he ran all the way home.

Chapter 18

On Friday morning, Dave returned to the hall at around 10AM. He found a welcoming committee made up of Jim, Anne and Harry waiting for him.

"Morning Dave," said Jim from his wheelchair. "You're late sunshine. You should have opened up half an hour ago. Final set preparations and all that!"

"I'm so sorry Jim. I overslept. Had a bit of a bad night, what with the, er, with your accident."

"It wasn't really a walk in the park for me either. In fact, a walk in the park might have been safer."

Dave unlocked the doors and they all went inside. Once they were safely in, Harry went up on the stage to finish off a spot of painting, whilst Jim and Anne cornered Dave.

"Dave, we've got a problem. I can't possibly perform as the ghost this evening, so we need someone else to do it. Someone who's seen the show. Someone tall, and almost as handsome as me. How would you feel about accepting the great honour of performing in the show?"

"Me? I'm no actor, Jim."

"Well that's OK, because at the moment, the important thing is that you have two legs that you can use to get around on the stage."

"I don't think acting is for me..."

"It could open doors for you."

"But the wind would blow leaves in and I'd have to sweep them up."

"No, not actual doors..."

"I don't know, Jim. I can't do it."

"There will be many pretty ladies in the audience watching, and they might want your autograph."

"Really?"

"Well, the will definitely be *some* ladies. And beauty is in the eye of the beholder, right?"

"Maybe then."

"I'll buy you a bottle of whiskey."

"Done."

They shook hands.

***

Harry finished the painting off whilst Anne sewed the last few hems and buttons that were required on the costumes. Jim kept Dave talking for quite a while, and otherwise only seemed to be at the hall to supervise, as there was not much else he could help with from the wheelchair.

The final touches were added to the set when Harry knocked some nails in to the scenery boards to hang a few pictures, and Chris turned up with a can of sparkly glitter paint, which he sprayed in liberal amounts over parts of the set where the ghost would be.

Dave took to the stage soon afterwards to run through a few scenes, and he did reasonably well. He had indeed being paying attention during rehearsals, and knew most of the lines by heart. But his posture left a lot to be desired, as he constantly slouched and leaned to one side.

Harry had an idea. "Dave, catch!" he said, throwing a broom to Dave. Dave caught it, and instantly stood perfectly straight.

"He's got a broom dependency!" yelled Jim.

"Well he can't wander around on stage with that during the performance, can he?"

The next few hours were spent teaching Dave how to stand without the support of a broom, with a half hour break for lunch at The Tavern.

Which turned in to a three hour break at The Tavern, where the food was good and the drink came quickly and often.

When Harry finally noticed the time, he managed to throw everyone in to a panic. There was so much left to prepare, and so little time left – the audience would be arriving in less than four hours, and Dave was still not quite ready.

And also, he may have been ever so slightly drunk.

"Right, everyone to their battlestations" said Harry. "This is war, and I intend to win. Even if this turns out to be the *Drunk Ghost Under the Stairs*, we have a show to put on!"

Chapter 19

The finishing touches were added to the set, the pictures were hung, the tablecloths put in place, the curtains straightened. Dave was dressed as the ghost, with a few alterations made to the costume that had been made for Jim. The fact that Dave was about a foot taller certainly did not help.

With half an hour left until the doors opened, Dave stood on the stage, looking decidedly unhappy.

Jim, Anne, Harry, Zoe and Sophie stood on the floor looking up at him, whilst the rest of the cast were backstage getting in to costume, makeup, and possibly character.

"THAT WILL NEVER DO."

"We don't really have a choice, do we?" said Jim.

"WAS MY AUDITION NOT GOOD ENOUGH FOR YOU?"

"What are you on about, Harry?"

"I didn't say anything, Jim."

"Oh, sorry Sophie. I thought it was Harry."

"Excuse *me*," said Sophie. "My voice isn't that deep!"

"PLEASE TURN AROUND, AND DON'T SCREAM."

They all turned and faced the shimmering blue ghost standing behind them.

"HELLO."

There was a bang from behind them, and Sophie turned back to look. "Dave! Are you OK?"

"HE'S FINE. HE DOES THAT QUITE A LOT. ALLOW ME TO INTRODUCE MYSELF. I AM ERIC BUTLER, ESQUIRE. BUSINESSMAN. POTATO MERCHANT. ACTOR. PLEASED TO MEET YOU."

The group mumbled *hellos*, trying not to look directly in to the ghost's face.

"IT'S OK. I DON'T BITE, DO I, ZOE?"

"He doesn't. I've met him before."

"I'D LIKE TO HELP OUT. I'VE PLAYED THE PART ALREADY, AS YOU'VE SEEN. AND IT WOULD BE AN HONOUR TO BE THE UNDERSTUDY TO MY GRANDSON."

"That's who you look like!" said Zoe. "Jim!"

Jim stared, mouth wide open. "You're my grandfather?"

"YES, AND FROM THE LOOK OF IT, I'M IN BETTER NICK THAN YOU, EVEN THOUGH I'M DEAD."

"Are you the one that's been going on about the toilets?" asked Harry.

"THAT IS I. BUT I NO LONGER NEED TO TAKE SOMEONE IN THE TOILETS. I FOUND SOMEONE TO REVEAL THAT WHICH WAS HIDDEN. BUT UNFORTUNATELY, IT SEEMS THEY WERE NOT AS PURE OF HEART AS I HOPED. THAT WHICH COULD HAVE SAVED YOU IS HIDDEN ONCE MORE."

"What are you on about?"

"I HEAR THE BUILDING IS TO BE SOLD. I TROD THE STAGE HERE FOR MANY YEARS, AND I'M NOT READY TO SEE IT GO. I HID MY FORTUNE IN THIS BUILDING, BUT DID NOT RECOVER IT BEFORE I DIED. AND NOW IT HAS BEEN RECOVERED, BUT HIDDEN AGAIN."

"What?"

*"**REALLY**? LONG STORY SHORT. I HID A*

GOLD CHAIN WORTH ABOUT HALF A MILLION QUID IN THE TOILETS, SOMEONE FOUND IT FOR ME YESTERDAY, AND THEY HID IT AGAIN. ONLY THE PUREST IN HEART WILL BE ABLE TO FIND IT NOW, SO I DON'T STAND A CHANCE. IF YOU HAD IT, YOU COULD BUY THIS PLACE IN AN INSTANT, AND THE SHOWS COULD GO ON FOR YEARS TO COME."

"So basically we're sitting on half a million quid, but you don't know where it is."

"THAT IS ABOUT THE SUM OF IT, YES. IT IS YOUR INHERITANCE, JIM. YOU ARE THE ONLY FAMILY I HAVE LEFT, BUT NOW I DON'T HAVE IT TO GIVE YOU."

"So why do you have to be pure of heart to find it?"

"OH, THAT'S SOME SUPERNATURAL REALM RULE. UNLESS THOSE WITH IMPURE HEARTS ARE DIRECTED ON HOW TO BEHAVE, THEY ARE NEVER OF CONSEQUENCE FOR GOOD. THE PURE HEARTS ALWAYS WIN THE DAY."

"Well, that rules Chris out then," said Harry. "Are you serious about going on stage?"

"OH YES. MY POWER HAS BEEN GROWING

OVER THE PAST FEW MONTHS. AS YOU CAN SEE, I AM NOW ABLE TO PROJECT A FULLY FORMED BODY. A WHILE AGO I WAS JUST A VOICE. A BOOMING, DELICIOUS, POWERFUL VOICE, BUT ONLY A VOICE. BUT MAY I ASK A QUESTION OF YOU?"

"Sure."

"ASIDE FROM MY REQUEST FOR YOU NOT TO SCREAM, WHY AREN'T YOU RUNNING AWAY IN FEAR? EVEN WHEN I TRY TO BE POLITE, MOST FOLK TURN AND RUN, OR PASS OUT LIKE DAVE THE BROOM MAN UP THERE."

"I think in my case, it's because I can't believe you are real." said Harry.

"SHAKE MY HAND." said the ghost, offering his right hand to Harry.

Harry went to shake the hand, and gasped as his own hand passed right through that of the ghost.

"BELIEVE IN ME NOW?"

Harry nodded, wide-eyed.

"GOOD. NOW LET'S GET ME INTRODUCED TO THE REST OF THE CAST."

***

Anne made a cup of tea for Dave, and sat with him while Jim· and Harry introduced Eric to the cast. Dave was pleased that he didn't have to perform in front of everyone, but more than a little concerned about how close he was to an actual living ghost. Or dead ghost, depending on how you looked at it.

Owen took it better than expected.

"So you're the little beggar who tried to get me in the toilets, eh? I've met your sort before. In a train station in Sheffield."

"OWEN!" snapped Sophie. "This is Jim's granddad. Be nice!"

"Well. If he's family, then that's OK. But there should still be a law against it."

"Against what?"

"Taking people in the toilet from beyond the grave."

Lillian smiled. "Hello again, Eric!"

"HELLO. HAVE WE MET ALREADY?"

"Yes! I think I was about 10. It was at the fair in

Blackworth."

"GOOD LORD! HOW CAN YOU REMEMBER SOMETHING SO LONG AGO? FOR THAT MATTER, HOW ARE YOU STILL ALIVE?"

"Looked after myself. You know what they say, a doctor a day keeps the apples away. Never did like cider."

"Moving quickly on," said Sophie, "this is Emily Ravenscroft."

"RAVENSCROFT? OF THE EDWINSTOWN RAVENSCROFTS?"

"I guess so...my gran used to live in Edwinstown."

"MY LADY! DO YOU NOT KNOW OF YOUR LINEAGE? IT IS AN HONOUR TO MEET YOU! ANYTHING YOU NEED, I WILL DO MY BEST TO BE OF SERVICE."

Eric made a motion as if to kiss Emily's hand.

"FORGIVE ME. I AM A LITTLE LESS SOLID THAN I WOULD LIKE TO BE."

"10 MINUTES TO CURTAIN!", yelled Jim.

"LOOKS LIKE I SHOULD GET READY."

"Do you need me to show you down to the

trapdoor?" asked Sophie.

"NO, MY DEAR. I DON'T NEED TO USE IT. I'LL BE ON STAGE AT ALL TIMES."

He gave a wink, and flashed out of existence. Another flash, and he was back.

"SEE?" he said with a smile.

***

Zoe took Chris to one side, skulking in the dark between the scenery boards.

"I know where the fortune is," she whispered.

"What? You'll have to get it! This would save the day! You must be pure of heart, and that evil Tom...I mean...your dad...will...er...sorry?"

"Here's what's going to happen. That night when I came round to see you, and I said I was falling for you, I was lying. I just wanted to drive a wedge between you and Sophie. But as it turned out, you stood up to me, and told me how you felt, for good or bad. And that, Chris, was *amazing*. No-one ever talks to me like that, because they all know who my dad is, and how powerful he is in this town. Everyone is a yes-man, but you showed some backbone, and I liked it."

"You like my backbone?"

"Something like that. So when all this is over and done, and the show is finished, you can take me out. You can take me out on Sunday night, when everyone else is celebrating a *job well done*, or more likely a *job poorly done*. I'm going to keep most of the fortune for myself, but I'll give you a bit, if you promise you won't try and save this place, and you take me out on a date on Sunday night. And now is not the time to have a backbone..."

"What if I say no? Then what, eh?"

"...like I said, now is not the time, Chris. You try and screw this up for me, and I'll tell Sophie that you invited me round and we did more than kiss. You get it?"

"I get it, I get it. Things are hard enough with Sophie right now anyway."

"And you think taking me out on a date will make it easier? No, because you're mine now. And we'll be rich together. Now get back in there, and act like nothing has happened."

"Whatever you say. You're the boss, now."

"Your backbone has melted."

Chris stood up straight. "I'm the boss, see, and I say I go back in there and don't say anything, you understand?"

"Yeah," said Zoe, rolling her eyes. "Whatever you say, *boss*."

Chapter 20

The lights dimmed, and the chatter of the audience quietened down. Around half the seats were filled, which showed that Lillian's campaign had worked – opening night was not normally so successful.

The PA system gradually faded in with the sound of heavy rainfall, and the lights flashed on and off at the sound of thunder. Slowly, the curtains drew back, revealing an empty stage. Zoe walked dramatically on, and took her place, centre stage.

"Oh lawks, what to do! Father is so ill, and may never recover, and the night is so full of strange noises. A creak here, a rattle there..."

The PA played the sound of a distant scream.

"...and the sound of a scream in the distance!"

Zoe's performance was masterful. The audience hung on her every word, and her actions were just over-the-top enough to convince even those sat at the back of her intent.

The story played out perfectly, and not a single name was mispronounced. In contrast to Murphy's Law, anything that could have gone right, did. The end of Act I drew near, and the party scene was nearly over. Sophie made her way in to the spotlight.

"...if only there were some way to know."

There was a loud bang, which caused the entire audience to jump, a flash of light, and there stood Eric the ghost on stage. Once again, tall and straight, confident. Shimmering light blue under the stage lights, and ever so slightly transparent.

The audience *oohed* and *aahed*. The effect was stunning.

"*My child*," said Eric. "*There is a way to know. You only have to ask the spirit world.*"

"Are you of the spirit world?" asked Sophie.

"*That I am. And I will show you wonders, such wonders. But now, come with me, and I will show you what you ask for!*"

Eric and Sophie left the stage, and the curtain dropped to rapturous applause.

During the interval, there was much texting and Twittering, and photos appearing online.

Seventeen new audience members arrived during the interval, each one purchasing a ticket at the door.

For the rest of the show, the audience sat in awe of Eric. A special effect that was so well done had never been seen in an amateur production, especially in Bentley Hill. Soon enough, Sophie was in the spotlight to deliver her final line to close the show.

"....and it all worked out in the end because of the ghost. The ghost from under the stairs!"

The audience rose as one to their feet, giving a standing ovation. The cast took a bow, one by one, with Eric bowing last. The ovation he received was deafening, and he couldn't help but grin.

When the applause eventually died down, Harry stepped forward.

"Thank you all for coming tonight, and don't forget to tell your friends if you enjoyed the show. We're here again tomorrow and again on Sunday. Thank you, good night!"

He gave a wave and the applause started again, and didn't stop even after the curtains had closed.

"That was fantastic!" said Emily.

"I think you're a hit," said Harry, smiling at Eric.

"*ALWAYS WAS, ALWAYS WAS. RIGHT, MUST DASH. BEING FULLY VISIBLE TAKES IT OUT OF YOU, SO I'M GOING FOR A NAP. SAME TIME TOMORROW?*"

"You betcha!"

***

Blackworth market was buzzing on Saturday morning with talk of the show the previous evening in Bentley Hill. No-one could believe how real the whole thing had seemed. Even with the ridiculous names, the audience had completely bought in to the story, thanks in no small part to that marvellous transparent man.

"I fink 'e's got mirrahs stuck on 'is coat. Thass why you can see stuff."

"Mirrahs don't let ya see froo fings!"

"Ah, mebbe. Mus' be windahs then. You can see froo windahs."

It seemed impossible to explain the ghost. The only logical explanation was that he was, in fact, a real ghost. And the town was not prepared to accept "it's a ghost" as a logical explanation.

Half an hour before the second show began, the hall was full. That is not to say that all the seats were taken – which they were – but more to say that the seats were filled, the standing room was occupied, and there was a queue outside. Some people were turned away due to safety concerns, but made sure they purchased front row tickets for closing night.

The second show was as good as the first, and a great cheer came from the audience when Eric appeared on stage. And just like opening night, he received the largest ovation at the end of the show.

By the time the final curtain came down, he seemed more transparent than ever.

"You alright there, gramps?" asked Jim.

"These shows are taking it out of me. I really need to rest. Unfortunately, it won't be eternal rest, as my fortune is still lost. But enough. I must go. I will see you all on closing night."

As Eric faded, a thought crossed Jim's mind. *By this time tomorrow, the Bentley Hill Players will be just as dead as Grampy Eric is.*

***

The final night of the show arrived, and for the second night running, the hall was packed to bursting. The show was once again perfect, not a word or action out of place – which was just as well, as Tom McLean had found himself a front row ticket, and nobody wanted to have any problems in front of Tom.

By the time the final ovations came round, Eric was very clearly transparent, and looked very tired. He took his bow, and the whole cast assembled in a line to take a bow together. As they shuffled around in to position, Sophie tripped over the hem of her long evening dress, and fell in to one of the side scenery boards. She desperately grasped at a picture hanging on the board to steady herself, but only succeeded in pulling it down with her. She landed with a thud, and the picture landed next to her with a distinct *thunk*.

The audience gasped, with the exception of Tom and Zoe, who were both struggling to stifle their laughter. Harry and Chris rushed to help Sophie back to her feet, while Eric looked on dumbfounded.

"...*I don't believe it. Jim, my boy, where are you?*"

"Right here!" said Jim from his position on the side of the stage. "Is she OK?"

"...*right as rain, I'm sure...but look!*"

They all looked at where Eric was pointing.

"...*it's your inheritance! The chain was holding the picture up!*"

"Whoa!" said Chris, picking the chain up. "This is heavy. Here you go Jim, it's all yours!"

"NO!" yelled Zoe. "I found it! It's mine!"

The cast turned to look at her. "You *found* it and didn't tell me?" asked Jim.

"Er...finders keepers, losers weepers. It was in my dad's building!"

"So are we, but we don't belong to him. Or you!"

"...*so the purest of heart found it. I'm so glad it's you, Sophie. You are...such a...nice...young lady...oh, I'm so tired...*"

Eric was nearly invisible by now. "...*the chain from the toilet is returned to my family...I can rest....in peace...thank you. Thank you all...I must rest...goodbye...*"

"Will we see you again?" asked Chris.

"...*good....b.....*"

And with that he was gone. The audience rose once again and gave another standing ovation.

Chapter 21

Tom McLean left his place in the front row and marched up on to the stage, and placed himself right at the front, in the centre.

"What a wonderful display, right there, it fair makes my heart ache. Absolutely sickening. Well I hope you folks have enjoyed the show, because it's the last one you'll ever see here!"

The audience started to boo. Someone threw a can of cola at Tom, which only just missed him.

"Just the sort of reprobates I expected here. This place is being sold at auction next Thursday, and will be torn down shortly after. The planning permission is in place for 'McLean Uptown Gardens", a new development of high class apartments. It's the only thing that's high class in Bentley Hill!"

The boos increased in volume, and more cans and packets of crisps were hurled towards Tom.

"Forget it! I'm selling it, and that's that!"

"No!", said Jim. "You most certainly are not selling it – at least not to any developers. That chain is worth more than enough to pay whatever price you are asking, and more importantly I checked it all out with the council on Friday. As a local community group, we get first dibs, and can put an offer in for the full asking price before the auction. And under the local by-laws, you'll have to accept the offer - this place is ours, sunshine."

"Even when you are stuck in a wheelchair, you still want to make my life hell. Why can't you just accept it?"

"Because these folk are like family to me. And Eric actually *is* family. Or at least, *was*. And looking after my family, and entertaining these good people in the audience, is far more important that any dodgy deal you have in mind."

The audience cheered.

"Whatever Jim. Have the damn place! As long as I get my money, you can turn the thing in to a home for disabled cats for all I care! Zoe, come on, we're going home!"

Zoe stepped up behind her father, and spoke in a hushed voice to him.

"Dad, don't embarrass me like this. It's not my

fault they got the chain. I thought I'd hid it well, and I was going to get it back before you sold up. And anyway, Chris is taking me out on a date tonight!"

"Actually, sweetie," said Chris. "I don't think I am. What you did could have ruined everything. And the way you tried to blackmail me too! Well, I can't forgive you for that. So I'm going to take someone on a date tonight, and I think we'll get a pizza. It's just not going to be you. Sophie, I need to tell you something. Zoe came over to my house one night and kissed me after we had that argument. But I threw her out. And she liked it. But more importantly, if you'll let me, I'd like to take you out tonight."

Sophie's eyes widened. "Of course I'll let you!"

"Like I said," said Tom, "Sickening. Good night, all. Actually forget the good. Forget all of you!"

He stormed off the stage, down the steps, and headed off in the direction of the exit.

"So will you come?" asked Chris.

"Sure. But you're paying though", Sophie laughed. "We're going to work this out, aren't we?"

"I think we already have," he said with a wink.

Zoe stamped her foot, and shook her fist at Christopher. "You'll be sorry!"

She ran off the stage to catch up with her father, who was already out the door.

"She *keeps* threatening me," said Chris. "I really don't think she likes me all that much."

Jim shook his head in despair at Chris, and cleared his throat. "Anyway, folks, sorry for that added bit of drama there. Can't say you don't get your money's worth at our shows! Thank you all for coming tonight. The money we've raised, in addition to the sale of this here chain, will ensure we can start work on our next production soon. And best of all, we'll still have somewhere to perform it!"

"Brilliant!", said Chris. "But after having a real ghost in *The Ghost Under The Stairs*, what can we do to top it?"

"Well, I don't know if we can top it, but we'll give it a go. The next production I've got in mind is called *The Death of an Actor*, and looks like it could be tremendous fun!"

"Remind me to check my life insurance," whispered Harry.

Curtain Call

Sophie and Chris enjoyed their date. They decided to take things slowly, but would definitely go out for pizza again. And maybe a movie.

Jim had the chain valued bright and early on Monday morning. By that afternoon, the Bentley Hill Players bank account was six figures better off. He put an offer in on the Bentley Hill Community Hall at 4 o'clock.

The offer was accepted by 10 o'clock on Tuesday morning, and The Players became the proud owners of the hall. There was enough cash left over to give the place a bit of a facelift, update the stage, and get a few new spotlights in, and some treats for the cast.

Owen managed to secure funding for a fresh bottle of gin, and a new bag to carry his things round in.

Lillian hoped to open a kissing booth, but settled for a box of cream cakes.

Emily wondered what the ghost had meant when he asked her if she knew of her heritage. The money wasn't going to help her find out, so she was left to wonder, and that was that. She did get a new jacket, though.

Dave received a new brush for his efforts.

And a power washer too, but the less said about that, the better.

Jim, Anne, and Harry formed a business together, and all became employees of said business. The main function of the business was to run the community hall and invest in whatever was needed to get any local amateur productions up and running.

Financially secure and with a permanent home, The Players were ready to put on a show again, and this time didn't need to employ the services of a ghost.

Which was lucky, as no-one saw Eric again.

And Zoe didn't get a horse.

But the chain for the toilet was finally replaced, so it all worked out in the end.

ABOUT THE AUTHOR

Adam G Newton was born in the East Midlands of England in 1975, and enjoys entertaining people and telling stories. He also enjoys drawing people with big noses.

He once won money in a competition on the back of a pizza box, and possesses a certificate that proves he knows how to search on Google.

He was once in a theatre group. And a band. At the same time.

He currently lives in Derbyshire with two teenage children and a dog, and writes for a variety of websites.

You can find him on Twitter:
@adamgnewton

And on his own website:
www.adamgnewton.co.uk

Printed in Great Britain
by Amazon